ANY MAN

In Memory of
Karen Smer
Ka ysz

ANY MAN

A Novel

Amber Tamblyn

HARPER PERENNIAL

NEW YORK • LONDON • TORONTO • SYDNEY • NEW DELHI • AUCKLAND

HARPER ● PERENNIAL

HarperCollins books may be purchased for educational, business, or sales promotional use. For information please email the Special Markets Department at SPsales@harpercollins.com.

FIRST EDITION

Designed by Jamie Lynn Kerner

Library of Congress Cataloging-in-Publication Data has been applied for.

ISBN 978–0–06–268892–7 (pbk.)

18 19 20 21 22   LSC   10 9 8 7 6 5 4 3 2

*Honey, don't take this the wrong way but
this book is dedicated to you.*

For David. My love.

ANY MAN

ONE

Am I in a body?

No body answers.

The sound of swallowing. A liquid click.
I feel a tongue.
Or a tongue is felt.
It is my tongue
or it is a tongue
belonging to someone else.
I am someone else.
Or I am the tongue
belonging to a self.

I am not a self.

I ask the tongue that is me
or the tongue that is in a mouth
to count.

How many teeth are left?

It doesn't want to.

Please.

The tongue lifts its twisted torso from the tonsils, thrown to the back of the throat like a child from a car's crash.

Darkness is a body.
I am in a darkness.
Or I am in a body.
A body is darkness.

The tongue searches, feels the teeth tremble like an ensemble of pebbles, disassembled. They are almost all accounted for. The tongue digs through an opening, touching air, past lips. My lips. Maybe. The tongue feels skin on a face.

What is feel?

No body answers

I open my eyes. The sky is a blue-cheese white with bullet holes of lapis, hued by the night's dethroning. A bird the size of the memory of a bird passes over like a spider falling perpendicularly. Someone shaped the clouds all wrong; splashed chum on the deck of dawn. Everything points away from itself. The abandoned skulls of nests rest in a nearby tree.

A woman approaches and stares down at me, her expression horror's portrait.

Can she see me?
Can I be seen?
Am I in a body?

She uncurls a thick scarf from her shoulders and lays it across me. Is it winter? There are no leaves on the trees. Is it cold out?

What is feel

The scarf's warmth is proof. Proof of pumped blood, of living. My living.
I am alive. In a body.

A trigger pulls and a seismic ache awakens. A searing pain rises, as the sun does, assured of its scorch. Every inch of me shakes.

She takes out a phone and dials quickly.
I laugh. The end of me tickles.

"He looks . . . Oh God, please get here quick . . ."

I am not dead. I am not not dead. I am in a body, on a ground, and it is morning. It is Winter or I am Winter. I am alive, at the behest of death's dress rehearsal. The pain. *The pain. Please.* My bones break each other, within. Internal ash. I move my jaw and it screams. Flex my toes and they scream. Tighten my anus, a scream. Swallow a scream. My legs are spread screams. I breathe—

"He's here in an alley outside the Green Tavern . . ."

—and the freezing air screams. Each rib expands and lets out a scream. I try not to breathe, which makes my heart scream. I take smaller screaming breaths instead. My sore neck screams as I try to lift it, making my back scream. My entire body unfolds.

The space between my hips does not scream.
Silence.
I reach a hand down to feel.
My hand feels, but what it's feeling
feels nothing.

"Yes, he's still breathing . . ."

Yes, I am still breathing.
No, I am not living.

Yes, I can feel my legs.
No, I cannot feel my genitals.

Yes, I can see.
No, I don't want to look.

Yes, Barack Obama.
March, I think. Early March. 2016.

Three fingers.
Donald Ellis.
Watertown. New York.
Yes, forty-seven years old.
Yes, an MFA in creative writing.
A poet.
No, I don't write anymore.
Yes, I teach kids.
No, I didn't mean to go to the bathroom while lying here.
No, I don't want to hang on.
Yes, I understand I will survive this.
No, I don't remember a face.
No, I don't know how this happened.
No, I don't want to cry.
Yes, I had some drinks.
Yes, I can still feel my legs.
No, I still can't feel my genitals.
Yes, I can see the church from the ambulance window.
No, I've never lost anything in the ocean.
No, I don't know what time the cemetery closes.
No, there was not enough room when we were kids.
No, it wasn't my mother's fault.
Yes, I feel alone.

Yes, I believe in God.

No, I do not want to pray.

Yes, I did see a ghost once when I was ten.

No, I can't remember the words to any songs right now.

Yes, everything is on fire.

No, I don't want you to put it out.

Yes, everyone's face is a blur.

No, I won't be hungry again.

Yes, I'm done with eating for the rest of my life.

Yes, I think the driver is humming something my grandmother used to.

No, she didn't tell me.

Yes, I think that's her in the car driving behind us.

No, she passed away years ago.

Yes, I understand I've lost blood.

Yes, I understand you may not be able to save it.

No, please don't give me the details.

No, I don't want to talk to the press.

No, I have no comment.

Yes, I understand I'm going to be fine.

No, I do not want to wake up after the surgery.

Yes, I'm still breathing.

No, I am no longer livable.

Yes, I'm a schoolteacher.

Yes, second-grade.

Yes, I'm married.

Camilla.

Fifteen years.

No, please don't call her. Don't tell her.

No, I don't want her to see me like this.

Yes, two. Amanda and Jake. Ten and seven.

Yes, I do. Very much.

Yes, I would like to cry now.

Yes, I understand.

Yes, I am scared.

Yes, I can still feel the pain.

No, please don't tell anyone.

No, I'm not ready.

Camilla sits next to my hospital bed, stained with the evening's abrupt catastrophe, half her black hair falling out of a hasty predawn bun, her shirt on backward and inside out. She's been up for two days straight, since they called and told her some woman found me lying in an alley. She tells me I was in surgery for several hours while they tried to save it, attempted to reconstruct it, get blood moving through it, figure out a way, with newer medical technology, plastic surgery even, to graft skin and salvage it, even if I might never be able to fully use it again. At least it would be there, in some way, nostalgia's souvenir. She tucks the curtains of her long bangs behind her ears and allows grief to take center stage. They were mostly unsuccessful, she says. We sink to the bottom of each other's oceans, drowning in shared silence. There are no pamphlets for this, no leaflets we can look through together about how to deal or move forward. Her green eyes pucker saltwater as she tells me it doesn't matter to her, that she'll love me no matter. I want to reach out and kiss her lids, run my thumbs over their creaminess and remember what delicate feels like. She holds my hand and says the local paper called me "an area man." She wants to know if I can believe that, like I don't have a name or something. When Camilla gets angry, her shoulders move back and forth as she speaks, like spreading wings. I've always

loved this about her. Sometimes I grab her by them and say, *Don't take off, hothead.*

The kids are with her mother. She thought it would be better to come alone so we could talk. There's a Detective Whirloch who wants to speak to me about the sexual assault when I get home from the hospital. *Sexual assault,* my brain repeats to my heart.

She unclenches her brow and kisses my palms, waiting for my response. A little part of me peels off and jumps out the seventh-story window. Besides the obvious, I've been treated for hypothermia, abrasions, and a little blood loss. They found high levels of Rohypnol in my system, she tells me. Is there anything I can remember, regardless? *Rohypnol, heart. Rohypnol.*

I tell her I remember a storm of moths fighting for a streetlight's attention. I remember the sound of a night bird not yet ready to quit. I tell her I remember a knee pushing against my throat, hairless and smooth. I remember a strawberry color moving electric overhead, a pink cloak dancing across my face.

I do not tell her what else is remembered.

Someone caressing the lobe of my ear with their tongue. A hand unbuckling my belt. The last hard-on I'd ever feel. Trying to stop it, then trying to stop stopping it. Rides of swinging nausea leaning in and out of my roller-coaster body. Guilt pulsing through every pore of my departing consciousness.

I do not tell her that I tried to stop it, because I can't remember if I did. I do not tell her what the person looked like, because I'm unsure. I do not say I enjoyed it, because I don't know if that's possible, given what happened, but if I did, she should leave me. I do not ask her if she's going to. I would understand if she did.

I want to pull my hand away from hers and never be touched again. I want to take off all my fingers like pen caps and write blood all over this room. I want her to loathe the man who could let this happen to himself, to have no pity, to tell me this is what I deserve. Her touch is a broken mirror in every room of my mind. Her touch is a tender, mistaken fool. I want to unscrew the entire arm she's got her hand on and just give it to her, let her have just that—my good, straight fingers, my thick pads, my forearms and sturdy wrists, unharmed. I want her to take the arm home and make it breakfast in the morning. Let the arm tie Amanda's shoelaces while she finishes packing Jake's lunch. Give it the car keys and let it drive everyone to school. I want her to send it dirty texts during lunch breaks. Make her smile and think only of gloves, daydreaming about manicures. I want her to crawl into bed next to it and stroke its elbow. Run her fingers over its cuticles. I want her to turn out the light and kiss the mouth of lines in its palm, happy and easy. Sleep there beside it, its wrist spooning her, its heavy, steady thumb draped over her ribs.

The rest of me will exit our picture's future. I'll go somewhere warm, black, and waterless, touching nothing, until she forgets my name.

Beep.

Hi baby, it's me.

It's about six thirty and I'm done with the staff meeting.

I swear Principal Sanders let out the most heinous, unchristly fart during the budget-cut meeting today.

I was sitting RIGHT next to him! And I couldn't say a word.

Had to watch him shovel a tray full of room-temp gouda into his mouth for two hours while that fart wrapped itself around me like, like . . . God, it was just awful.

Listen, I'm going to meet Mark for a couple beers at the Green Tavern

and maybe a bite since the kids are doing that sleepover thing?

And I know you'll be out late at that baby-shower thing, right?

I just said "thing" twice.

Anyway, tell Jessica I say hi.

Call me back if any of that's a problem.

Also, I can pick them up in the morning if you want to sleep in. The kids.

Maybe I'll get some of those breakfast burrito thingies you always get.

Are those from Joe's Café? And is Jake still doing the vegetarian thing?

Okay, Jesus, this message is way too long, we can figure it out in the morning.

Honey, why did you marry me? I talk a lot.

Love you.

Bye.

"My name's Detective Whirloch, but you can call me Myles, okay?

"Would you like your wife to join us, Mr. Ellis?

"I'm going to have to ask some tough questions, so if at any time you want to stop, let me know and we will, okay?

"My first priority is your mental well-being, understood?

"What time did you arrive at the Green Tavern on the night of March second?

"Were you alone, or were you with any friends prior to meeting the offender?

"Do you mind if I get contact information for your friend Mark?

"Did you know any other people at the bar that night?

"Is there anyone you know personally who's been volatile toward you lately?

"Do you remember how you first came into contact with the offender?

"Do you remember any facial features of the offender?

"Anything specific about the offender, such as hair color or moles on the body?

"Do you recall anything the offender said to you before or after the assault?

"Do you ever think about what the offender might be feeling, Mr. Ellis?

"Aren't you ashamed of yourself, Mr. Ellis?

"What are you going to do if the offender is someone you know?

"What are you going to say to the offender when you see them in court?

"Do you think everyone will look at you differently now?

"Do you have any clocks in your house, and how many clocks do you own?

"Have they ever all simultaneously stopped?

"Do you think you'll sleep okay in the coming decades?

"Do you think this is your fault, Mr. Ellis?

"You do, don't you, Mr. Ellis?

"What will Camilla think of you?

"How are you going to tell your children?

"Are you interested in assisted suicide as an option?

"Have you ever heard of the kamikaze birds of India, Mr. Ellis?

"Did you know horned lizards can squirt blood out their eyes?

"Do you intend to recover from this fully?

"Is there a word for what you're feeling?

"What would your father think of you if he were still alive?

"Are you going to cry?

"Do you believe in purgatory?

"Have you ever heard wolves howl in a place where wolves do not reside?

"Do you recall how many alcoholic drinks you had that evening?

"What force was threatened or used by the offender, if you know?

"Do you recall physically resisting at any time during the assault?

"Can you remember anything you said to the offender over the course of the night?

"What can you tell me about the chronology of sex acts that were performed?

"Did you perform any sex acts, including kissing, before the assault took place?

"Would you like to take a break, Mr. Ellis?

"Would you like some water?

"Would you like the number to a crisis center here in town?

"Would you like references for therapists who work with this kind of trauma?

"Let's pick this back up once you're back home, okay with you, Mr. Ellis?"

Camilla rolls me in a wheelchair down a Listerine-reeking hospital hallway toward the elevator. It's easier this way, they tell us. It will be painful for me to walk for a few weeks. I can't lift my eyes to meet those of the nurses, patients, or doctors as I go. I can feel them. I am a damaged relic leaving the museum for good. I stare at their shoes. Patent leather. Slip-ons. Wedges, I think they call them. Sneakers. Even high heels. All those better, happier feet.

"What would you like for dinner, Don," Camilla asks. Light talk is as good as any other way to begin my death sentence.

"Steak? Lasagna?"

All food is a last meal.

"Fish?"

Everything leads to the execution.

I'll have the fish, please, and Camilla my dear, can we swing by the bar on the way home I think I left my body there

The elevator doors open and a woman and her husband step out, carrying flowers and balloons bearing the words "Get well!" She stops at the sight of me, gasps, and halts her husband with a hand to his chest.

"I'm sorry . . . are you . . . Donald Ellis?"

No, ma'am, but I get that all the time.
You must've mistaken me for a butcher's block.
You must've mistaken me for a skinned deer.
You must've mistaken me for some coward.
Donald is no longer with us.
Donald died reading a poem to a bullfighter.
Donald was scratched to death by a peacock.
Donald passed away trying to make love two hundred meters under the ocean.
Donald left this world chiseling turquoise out of rock with his bare hands.
Donald's fingers bled to death.
Donald swallowed one hundred matches and rubbed his body against a volcano.
He died instantly.
Donald got into an argument with the moon and died instantly.
Donald revealed how much he could love and died instantly.
Donald met his friend for a beer after work and died instantly.
Donald has to explain to his children what happened and will die instantly.
Donald will touch his wife's thigh and die instantly.

"I just want to say it's so awful what happened to you—you're all over the news!—but just, like, know that everyone is on your side and sending you prayers . . ."

Donald dies instantly

". . . I'm so sorry to ask, but would you mind if I got a selfie with you?"

TWO

A MAN NAMED DONALD RETURNS TO A HOUSE WITH a wife after seven days in a hospital. Donald carries a plastic bag filled with personal items given back to him after he was discharged. Donald enters a house where, it's said, he's resided for over a decade. Donald finds the belongings and stranded activities of children scattered around the living room, as if they were kidnapped right in the middle of what they were doing. Donald has no recollection of the house. Donald has no recollection of its potted plants. Donald has no recollection of its smell. He sees framed photographs of children and a wife all over the living room. He sees a framed master's degree for a man named Donald. Perhaps Donald once dreamed of becoming a famous novelist or poet. Donald now dreams of nothing. For he is a no one.

Donald sees a slice of bread dropped on the floor next to the kitchen table, sees that all the lights have been left on, sees paintbrushes sitting in a glass full of foggy paint water. The house looks more like a museum of a life than the longtime home of a man named Donald. Donald has no recollection of the man named Donald who he sees in a mirror. Donald has no recollection of the staircase in the house and where it leads. Donald has no recollection of breath. He takes a long time to ascend the stairs, counting each one as he goes. Donald has no recollection of what comes after five. Donald seems to recall seven but can't be sure. In a bedroom, Donald cannot identify personal items. Donald opens a sock drawer to find that it is actually a sweater drawer. He swears it's always been a sock drawer. He tries to sit on the bed in the bedroom but it hurts to sit, so he just stands in the middle of the bedroom that belongs to a man named Donald. He sets the bag of personal items from the hospital on a nearby dresser and sees another framed photo of children. These must be the children of the man named Donald, as he's seen them all over the house. Donald notices a dark figure standing in the background of the photograph. Some creature with a wild, tangled mouth. Some ghost. Fear surges through Donald's body as he worries for the safety of the children in the photograph. Donald blinks and realizes it is just Donald in the photograph with the children, not a ghost. Donald takes the photograph out of the frame and looks closer to make sure. Yes. It's just a man. A creature, still. He places the photograph on the carpeted floor of the bedroom. Donald takes a wallet out of the hospital bag and puts it in the medicine cabinet in the bathroom. Donald removes the reading glasses from the hospital bag and drops

it out the second-story window. Donald takes out a watch and places it in the shower. Donald is settling in just fine. The hospital did not include Donald's personal clothing in the hospital bag, perhaps because it is evidence now. Donald is evidence now. Donald retrieves the last of the items and places them on the floor with the photograph of the children and the creature. Donald enters a closet filled with the belongings of a man and begins pulling out all of his belts. There are many of them. Donald places the belts on the floor with the other items; a bed of snakes. They move. Donald quickly retrieves a lighter and lights the den of them on fire. Donald has no recollection of burning. Donald has no recollection of objects. Donald has no recollection of pain. Donald watches as the carpet around him begins to smolder. Soon the carpet is also on fire. The smoke in the bedroom sets off a loud alarm and triggers a sprinkler system in the ceiling. Water rains from the stucco. Donald recalls a thunderstorm when he was a child that killed a local dog. Donald recalls leaning over a railing in the arms of his mother and running his young hand under a waterfall. Donald recalls learning how to swim. Donald recalls the dark woods. Twigs piercing into his back under the pressure from above. Donald recalls the above. Donald drowns. The room burns as a woman screams a man's name from downstairs.

Donald! What's going on up there?

Donald what's going on?

Donald

Donald

DONALD

I sit in front of my therapist, Irene, once a week. I do not talk, or I talk about the news, the Olympics, the different kinds of charcoals one might use for barbecuing; I talk about landscaping, the sculptures of Koons, the vegetables I'm pissed they were out of at the farmers' market. I do not talk, or I talk about old wars, my daughter winning first place at the science fair, my son's slipping grades. I talk about the origin of toothpaste, which I've read has a Nazi connection. I talk about Rachmaninoff, my desire to go horseback riding someday, my disdain for the Green Party. I do not talk, or I talk about seeing the Hells Angels come through town once, I talk about my desire to see the Grand Canyon, I talk about having no desire to see Mount Rushmore. I talk about Camilla's successful recent eye exam, the best ways to store fresh herbs in the fridge, the Mets, the new Chinese restaurant that opened up in town, the weather. I talk about the prose of Anne Carson or the plays of Chekhov. I talk about spending my twenties aspiring to be a writer that was somehow a combination of the two. I talk about the new line of razors I've discovered, the different uses for valerian root, the stupid closure on the 20 that made us late for my follow-up doctor's appointment. I talk about *Judge Judy*, my new favorite TV show; I talk about physical therapy; I do not talk. I do not talk, or I talk about the invention of the rocking chair, mutts versus purebreds, the health benefits of sunflower seeds, the new bristleless broom I ordered off Amazon. I talk about the walking shoes I just purchased, the best brands of mosquito repellent, the time I was mutilated and left for dead in an alley, the time I went rafting with friends for my forty-sixth birthday. I do not talk. I do not talk. I do not talk. I do not talk. I do not talk. I do not talk. I do not talk. I do not

talk. I do not talk. Or I talk about the effects of wind on different sizes of birds. I talk about taxidermy. I talk about golf.

THREE

"WELCOME BACK, MR. ELLIS, WE MISSED YOU!" READS one of the dozens of cards cluttering my classroom desk, where I haven't sat in over four weeks, since what happened happened. Every condolence cake, every overstayed sympathy hug or half-assed buck-up-buttercup smile is another reminder of how much I've disappeared. Am disappearing. I shove the cards and a bouquet of flowers into my desk drawer. I move slower now. I have to. Walking is very hard for me. Some days the pain is so bad, I can't sit, either. I just have to stand, wherever I am, without moving. Amanda and Jake call it "statue time," standing alongside me in cafés or on a street corner. I tell them Daddy is just thinking, he needs to stop to think. They are happy to play this game with me. It's safer for their imaginations if they

do. They still see how slowly I put on my shoes, how I'm careful when bending over. The measured unease of getting in and out of our car or climbing stairs in a building with no elevator. There is no game in that.

I've arrived almost two hours before class so I can prepare. It is my new routine. Sometimes I'll arrive at an appointment three hours early just so I have time to stare out my car window. I watch and try not to think. Everything is a film: a fly on the windshield trying to get in, a delivery truck parked in front of whatever to deliver something I will never savor, a plane carrying flesh messages across the sky. The movie is wonderful to watch when I'm not in it.

The early-arrival routine also allows for time to practice smiling in the rearview. I tilt it toward me until I can see only my mouth. At home, I do the same. When I get out of the shower and wipe the fog off the glass, I check the stubble on my chin, clean my ears, staring at the lobes. But I avoid my eyes. Always. I run my fingers through my wet hair and consider its line, receding like a riverbank in a drought. When my daughter, Amanda, calls me into her bedroom to ask which outfit she should wear to school, holding each pair of overalls up to her small chest, I look her in her eyes in the full-length mirror and tell her I love the blue one with the sea otters on it. I am not afraid of my daughter's eyes. At the front door, I check my tie, my collar, and the nick on my chin from my razor. I check my brows, even, and am able to wipe the crusts off my lids without looking directly into my own eyes. Every once in a while, though, it happens, and I'll catch them by sheer proximity. My pupils are stabbed into my head like black thumbtacks pinning my entire face in place. My eyes are no

38

longer a part of my body. We do not know each other. I see them, but they do not see me.

The rearview in my car is the best mirror to practice my smiling because it's small. I can focus on the one part of my face I'm intending to, and see nothing else. I start with one side of my mouth, lifting the invisible strings of my lips, then dropping them back into resting. I lift the other side, half smiling, and drop it back. Half smile, rest. Half smile again, rest. Then I lift both at the same time, slowly, spreading the meat halfway across my face like a loving bow. The human smile no longer makes sense to me. Why is it a sign of happiness? Who decided that? Why not the crinkling of the nose, or blinking, or a hard swallow? Who invented the word *smile* and gave it its meaning? Smile is the shape of my mouth Amanda wants to see when she comes running out of the science fair, pushing her lime-colored glasses up her nose and shrieking with good news. Smile is the shape of my mouth my therapist looks for when she asks how I'm doing. It is the shape of my mouth Camilla wants to kiss when I return from a day's work. The shape of my mouth my neighbors and colleagues desire to set them at ease. It makes others feel safe with my story. I practice this smiling, this mouth's shaping, in the mirror. I do it for them.

"MORNING, DONNIE," MY COLLEAGUE EUGENIA, A TENURED, ECCENtric boil of a woman, says, sticking her shriveled head in and rapping loudly on my door. She teaches math in the special-ed department and eats mustard on bread—not toast—every day for lunch. Eugenia isn't known for her warmth, which garnered her the nickname Genie the Meanie from some of the

first graders, and it caught on with some of the adult staff, as well. Genie the Meanie wears patterned tights with Crocs and jean vests still pinned with buttons from the '60s. She always paints her nails a bright hooker red and wears no makeup. The faculty spend their lunch breaks gossiping about Eugenia over home-prepared salads with dressing on the side.

I wave her in and put on the shape of my mouth I've been practicing.

"How are you doing, son?" she asks, her bangles clanging on her wrists as she drops a wrinkled paw onto my shoulder. It is the most common question I am asked, and I know everyone wants to hear only one answer.

"Good," I say.

"Bullshit."

I look up from my desk.

"You're not good, Junior, but that's okay, you will be. You're a damn mess, I can see it on you."

I play with my tie.

"Don't worry, son, no one else can see it. You're not good right now, but you will be."

She pats me hard, her cigarette-and-Dijon breath crawling down my throat.

"Thanks," I say, "appreciate it."

The bell rings.

Genie the Meanie marches out.

"Hey! No running in the halls, you bunion!"

I've arrived an hour and ten minutes early to Irene's office.
I move the rearview. I practice the shape of my mouth.
I take a deep breath and do my staring.
I watch the movie play around me.

I think about my students. Today's class. Their easy eyes
welcoming me back. The big meadows of their minds, open.
The grief loosens its jaw from my neck but doesn't let go.
Jimmy Hillstein, a quiet redhead who lost his father in a truck-
ing accident when he was five, stayed seated in the back of the
room. Jimmy developed a bad stutter over the year following
his dad's death and soon stopped speaking altogether. Speech
therapy helped him find his voice again, mostly through singing. In class, he would raise his hand and sing his answers
to me. His brave alto would push out words to the tune of
"Yellow Submarine": "It-wasn't-Columbus but Leif-Er-ikson,
Leif-Er-ikson." He sang a lot of answers in this tune, getting
creative with syllables and consonance to make each one fit
the melody. It wasn't just Jimmy's ability to bloom in the face
of such pain that got to me but also the tenderness of his
fellow students. They never made fun of Jimmy's silence or
his stutter or his singing answers, ever. I understand Jimmy's
fragility. My father died in an accident when I was a teenager,
though I dealt with my grief less quietly. We stared at each
other from across the classroom. He got up and adjusted his
shirt so his belly wouldn't peek out from underneath. He came
to my desk and squinted. He handed me a note.

"How was your first day back, Donald?" Irene asks after I
do not talk.

Yes, I am still breathing.
No, I am not living.
Yes, I can feel my legs.

"I've been putting on a good face, Irene. Each day grows toward its death. I try to forget. Forgive. Every day I die again. My family lives a life of burial. Everything makes me want to cry. Everything makes me angry. Everything makes me numb. Repeat. I'm tired. Paranoid. I'm cold most of the time, wearing full sweaters in the hot spring."

No, I cannot feel my genitals.

"I've had to relearn how to go to the bathroom. I'm still wearing a catheter. I can't make love to my wife. I fake it with my children. There is no difference between meanings anymore. A cereal bowl is a pillow is a trash bin is a knife is a fistfight on the street."

Yes, I can see.

"I can't stop thinking about what I could've done to stop it that night."

"I'm listening."

"I went into the bar to meet my friend Mark for some drinks. It was a Wednesday. He left early to meet his wife for dinner. I struck up a conversation with someone. They say I left the bar alone. They say someone entering the bar saw me

and said I looked disoriented. Someone . . . the offender . . . was outside. Maybe they had been inside? Watching me? I felt dizzy. I needed to sit down. The offender took me out into the woods. I ended up in the grass under the trees, though no one knows how I got there. They said my pants were taken off. I was barely conscious at that point. Sedated. I couldn't stop the—I couldn't do anything . . ."

No, I don't want to look.

"My arms were held down, I was too weak to struggle. My legs pinned. Barely conscious. The offender . . . The offender rubbed back and forth on top of me, with . . . clothes still on. With thick, rough jeans. The offender rubbed against me until . . . Until there was nothing left of me. Until every part of me, below . . . was destroyed.

Yes, I am still breathing.

"I was dragged back to the Green Tavern and left there in the freezing cold, behind the building, next to the trash. Without my clothes on. Covered in blood. The offender . . ."

No, I am not living.

A long silence. I can no longer speak.

A demon reaches into my mouth and rips out all the bells.

Sobered, angry, wordless, impossible to explain, explosive, remorse-hung, humiliated into morbidity. My life. *My life.* Smeared across the wall like feces in a ward. I weep. Wipe

snot and tears away from my face and grind my knuckles deep into the suede of Irene's couch, sweat forming, my ass levitating off the cushions with a pulsing shame. I want to smash my many hearts against a spike. I want to run. I give in. Give in to my skeletal now, my peachless unease. "The offender," I call my attacker, ashamed. I cry so hard I have to adjust the tube connected to my urine bag so as not to pinch it. I lean forward and hold one hand on the tube and the other hand over my face. This face I used to own, cawing a boy's breaking, my entire body trembling in its zero-foot, life-sentenced cell.

"May I sit next to you, Donald?"

"Yes."

Dear Mr. Ellis,

Today my mom made me pancakes because it is a special day because you are my favorite teacher and you are back and that makes me happy. My mom made one of the pancakes in the shape of an E for Ellis. If you ever want to talk to me about what happened and why you had to go away Mr. Ellis I will listen and I will be your friend. My best friend is Rotty my dog and he always listens to me whenever I am sad. I can be your Rotty if you need one. My mom says a bad thing was done to you by a bad person they can't find and it was on the news. But I don't care about the news. I only care about you.

Your friend,
Jimmy

P.S. I also care about Rotty too. And mom.

Jake's hunched over a painting on the front porch, surrounded by a clutter of pastels, when I pull into the driveway. I was planning on sitting in the car for a while to shake off the session with Irene, but the sight of my son softens me. He is markedly different from his older sister, the science lover with a social magnetism and flair for fluorescent fashion. His sister will one day be working on launchpads for NASA and marry some Pulitzer Prize winner. Jake is my introspective artist, my quiet landscape navigator, my insect whisperer.

"Hey, you."
"Hey, Dad."
"What are you working on there?"
"Just a drawing."
"Ah. Nice. Of what?"
"Just a thing."

I nod, rest my chin on my hand, my elbow on the car window frame.

Jake rubs his nose, speaks without looking up from his painting.

"What are *you* working on in there?"
"Just sitting in the car, Monkey. Nothing special."
"Oh."

"Want to go for a drive?"

"Do you want to go down to the river?"
"Sure."

46

"How was school today?"

"I don't know, kind of fun, I guess."

"Oh, yeah? Tell me."

"Well . . . well, I found a salamander at lunch."

"Yeah?"

"Yeah."

". . . And?"

"And it felt funny in my hands. The skin. But I petted it, right there between the eyes, ya know? Like a cat?"

"Yeah . . ."

"Yeah, and it fell asleep in my hand. That was kinda cool."

"Sounds like it."

"Yeah."

"How long did it sleep for?"

"Long enough that I could kinda sketch it a little."

"Oh yeah? Is that what you were working on at the house?"

"No, that was this other thing."

"Gotcha. Okay."

"Buddy, take off your sandals if you're going to put your feet on the dash."

"Sorry. Okay."

"Don't be sorry, Monkey."

"There should be parking coming up . . ."

"Okay . . ."

"So . . ."

"Yeah, Monkey?"

"Do you feel funny since you got home?"

"What do you mean?"

"You're just sorta quiet, I guess. I don't know."

"I know. It won't be like this for long, I promise."

"Okay . . ."

"Is there anything else you want to ask me, Monkey?"

". . . I don't know."

"Have people been saying things to you at school?"

". . ."

"Jake, listen . . . listen to me, don't cry, Monkey. Don't cry. Listen . . . I'm here, aren't I? I'm alive and fine and here."

"I know . . . it's just . . ."

"What? You can tell me."

"I don't know . . ."

"Okay. You don't have to share anything if you don't want to. But know I'm fine. Really, I am. I'm here, okay? I'm here."

". . . It's just, some people called you bad names that I didn't like. And asked me how you could . . . could . . ."

"Could what, Monkey?"

"Could get . . . raped . . . and I didn't even know what that word was. I had to look it up. It sounds so bad. Is that what happened to you?"

". . . It's complicated, Jake. It's really complicated. But . . . let me try and explain it to you . . ."

". . ."

"Some people in the world are bad people. What happened to me . . . I was kind of like that salamander . . . asleep for what happened to me."

"But why were you sleeping?"

"Well . . . one of the bad things that happened was, some-

one put something in my drink that made me very, very sleepy. So it didn't hurt me. I couldn't feel anything."

"Why did you let someone put something in your drink?"

"I didn't *let* that happen, Jake . . . It was put in my drink when I wasn't looking."

"Oh. . . . But why weren't you looking, Dad?"

"Jake, buddy, listen. Listen to me. What matters is I'm fine now and they're going to find that bad person so they can't do bad things to other people. Do you believe me?"

"Yeah."

"Okay, kiddo. Let's get out here and sit by the water, sound good?"

"Yeah, okay."

We sit hip to hip, overlooking Black River Bay. I put my hand around his narrow shoulders and hold him close. I'd grow extra mouths to swallow all his confusion and sorrow. We say nothing. The clouds move the wind, flirt the trees, gust the water, caress the fish, tickle the reeds, polish the stones, suckle the moss, gurgle the river, choir the valley. Somewhere a salamander sleeps. Somewhere an owl opens one eye. Somewhere a bad thing, somewhere a good thing, no thing, and everything. The air cracks its warm clarity against our hair. The smell of grilling meat wafts by us. I love him. I will protect him.

Yes, I am still breathing.
No, I am not living.

FOUR

LOCK THE DOOR BEHIND ME. IT'S EASIER TO GET READY FOR BED
when I'm in the bathroom alone. I lower the lights until I
can barely see. I undo my buckle and unzip my pants. I hate
the sound of a zipper's descent. I carefully pull the waist-
band of my slacks down over my hips while also bellowing
the fabric, slowly pulling like a flag to half-mast, making sure
nothing snags the bag of piss clinging to my thigh. I step out
of the puddle of fabric on the floor one leg at a time, mindful
not to pull my wrapped leg up too high and pinch the catheter. Naked, I un-Velcro the bag from my leg and disconnect it
from its tube. I prop it up on a towel next to the sink. I wash
my hands for fifteen seconds with soap. I remove the bag's
drain spout from its sleeve and open it. I spread my legs and
stand over the toilet. I hold its head, now a Picasso of pigment,

and lean its misshapen body over the bowl with one hand. With my other hand, I pick up the bag of urine. I look up at a shelf filled with Camilla's eye creams. *Honey, why did you marry me?* I do not look down as I turn the urine bag upside down into the toilet bowl and enjoy the familiar trickle against porcelain. I close my eyes. I remember. I imagine.

I'm holding a perfect lever.
A skin-sheathed cleaver. A velvet coffer.
I'm holding a bag of a hundred warm nickels.
The steeple on a sun-soaked sandcastle.
I'm holding a newborn baby eagle,
A portrait of Poseidon on an easel,
a hawk moth larva,
a miniature statue of the Dalai Lama.
I'm holding Mr. Potato Head,
Van Gogh's big beautiful ear,
a gourd,
a gun,
I'm holding a fresh-cut cow's tongue.
I'm holding a mountain with a lenticular cloud,
a swarm of sleeping starlings before dusk.
A tarantula's cocoon,
an inverted maelstrom,
a titan arum blossom.
I'm holding a throbbing tornado.
A monarch's libido.
A calcified bird from Lake Natron.
The horn of a Watusi bull.
A king's skull.

A shard from a broken crystal ball.
A famous scroll.
I'm holding timber from the Black Forest.
I'm holding a whale's vein.
I'm holding my father's hand.
I'm holding my father's name.

In the morning, the air is thick with the smell of cooked onion and coffee. Someone has slid a piece of paper underneath the bedroom door. A painting. Jake's. In the painting, a man and a boy sit on a dock overlooking a river and a forest. The sun shines brightly from above, illuminating each leaf in shades of green, yellow, and gold. The man wears a crown. He does not smile, but his body does. The man isn't holding the boy with arms but with wings, long and strong. The boy's eyes are closed. He does not see, but his body does.

Beyond them, a thick curtain of green trees is drawn. Between the parted woods, a small pair of black eyes peer out and a misshapen scribbled hand claws at the bark, its other arm long, dragging in the mud.

The creature is headless.

It moves.

Downstairs, I find Camilla frozen in the kitchen, staring at the television as onions burn on the stove.

"Authorities are confirming that a man identified as Pear O'Sullivan has been brutally attacked and assaulted in Springfield, Massachusetts . . ."

It moves.

It—

". . . Investigators believe the perpetrator is likely the same person who attacked Watertown schoolteacher Donald Ellis just three months ago. A perpetrator who authorities now believe is an unidentified woman."

55

She.

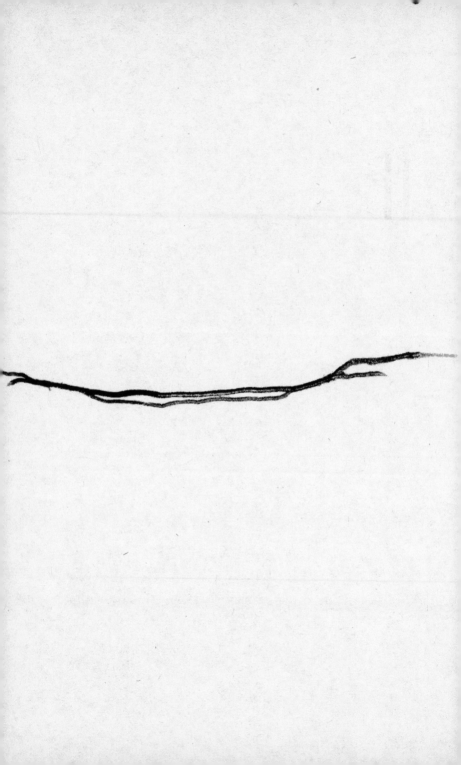

ONE

<You are now chatting with JasmineRose.>

JAMARVELOUS83: Yo

JASMINEROSE: Hey there

JAMARVELOUS83: Jamar here. Is yours Jasmine or Rose? Or both?

JASMINEROSE: Jasmine though some people call me Rose too

JASMINEROSE: Where are you from, Jamar? I like that pic of you. The profile one.

I guess that's why we're talking tho right? lol

JAMARVELOUS83: LOL yeah. Same about your pix. You mixed? Can't really tell . . .

JASMINEROSE: Yeah you?

JAMARVELOUS83: Yeah. West Indian pops. Irish hippie mom.

JASMINEROSE: Nice

JAMARVELOUS83: Is it?

JASMINEROSE: lol

JAMARVELOUS83: How long have you been on Cupid? This place is kind of weird.

JASMINEROSE: lol super weird. Not long enough to feel comfortable with it.

JAMARVELOUS83: Yeah I've been on for 6 months. It's got its upsides.

JAMARVELOUS83: It's usually a mixed bag you know?

JASMINEROSE: lol Yeah

JAMARVELOUS83: But fuck all that. Tell me about yousilf

JAMARVELOUS83: *Yourself! Shit. That wasn't even an autocorrect

JASMINEROSE: lol

JAMARVELOUS83: It's like they set these things up to deliberately sabotage any game a dude might have

JASMINEROSE: lol

JASMINEROSE: no worries

JASMINEROSE: I'm from Wichita originally

JASMINEROSE: Are you familiar at all?

JAMARVELOUS83: Of course! Are you kidding? They have the best

JAMARVELOUS83: (runs and googles Wichita real quick)

JASMINEROSE: Ha1

JASMINEROSE: !

JAMARVELOUS83: . . . Interactive children's events aaaaaaaaand . . .

JASMINEROSE: haha

JAMARVELOUS83: . . . Plains, I guess?

JASMINEROSE: haha yeah we're well versed in the world of wide open spaces

JAMARVELOUS83: Okay now you're just straight up FLIRTING with me, quoting Dixie Chicks

JASMINEROSE: lol ya got me

JAMARVELOUS83: So Wichita . . .

JASMINEROSE: So yeah then I moved to New York to work in . . . wait for it . . .

JAMARVELOUS83: . . .

JASMINEROSE: Insurance.

JAMARVELOUS83: Let's get married.

JASMINEROSE: haha

JAMARVELOUS83: I've never heard such a touching story

JASMINEROSE: But wait there's more!

JAMARVELOUS83: I don't care. I'm in. For life. No prenup.

JASMINEROSE: haha

JASMINEROSE: Sounds like a plan

JASMINEROSE: Where did you go to school?

JAMARVELOUS83: Syracuse Uni. Live in Albany now.

JASMINEROSE: Nice. What did you study?

JAMARVELOUS83: English. Can't you tell?

JASMINEROSE: Oh yeah for sure I haven't seen a single Oxford comma!

JAMARVELOUS83: You are funny, sexy, and come from the plains.

JASMINEROSE: haha there it is!

JASMINEROSE: I'd like to use that on my epitaph

JAMARVELOUS83: Well don't die YET, we have a lot of kids to have, and a mortgage to fight over

JASMINEROSE: haha ugh

JAMARVELOUS83: And mothers-in-law to complain about and a withering sex drive to
blame for our porn addictions

JASMINEROSE: Oh God this is so intense for a first convo

JAMARVELOUS83: Arghhh sorry I was just trying to be funny.

JASMINEROSE: No I know . . . you are a very funny guy for sure. Tell me more about you.

JAMARVELOUS83: Cool. In a nutshell I was born and raised in upstate NY. I love baseball. I'm 36 and share a birthday with my favorite writer, J. D. Salinger. After college I kind of fell into web design by accident.

JASMINEROSE: lol how do you "kind of fall into" that line of work?

JAMARVELOUS83: It's pretty embarrassing but basically I was trying to build a website for myself as I was considering getting into acting and I read somewhere you need a good headshot and a good website.

JASMINEROSE: Ha! Really?

JAMARVELOUS83: Yes. In all honesty, I got high one night and watched Turner Classic Movies and thought, "Hey, I could do that"

JASMINEROSE: That is hilarious

JAMARVELOUS83: I wanted to be Cary Grant but instead I discovered I was Steve Wozniak. (Which is also a great name for my future memoir.)

JASMINEROSE: Oh wow. I know nothing about that stuff. Who is Steve Wozniak?

JAMARVELOUS83: The less famous guy who also founded the company Apple.

JASMINEROSE: Oh wow

JAMARVELOUS83: Yep. So yeah, English major to attempted actor to computer coder to semi-loser!

JASMINEROSE: ha

JAMARVELOUS83: My work revolves around being online a lot of the time so naturally a lot of my personal life is also spent and enjoyed here too. Online.

JASMINEROSE: How so?

JAMARVELOUS83: Well . . . here we are, aren't we?

JASMINEROSE: Yeah but that's not because you choose to, right? I mean none of us CHOOSE this

JAMARVELOUS83: mmm yes and no, for me

JASMINEROSE: We are on here because it's hard to meet people in person nowadays with our jobs and lives

JASMINEROSE: Why do you say "yes and no" for you

JAMARVELOUS83: I say it because this type of interaction—that we're having right now—is more fun. Ya know? Online. Doesn't come with any baggage and you can talk to lots of people.

JASMINEROSE: Huh.

JAMARVELOUS83: Yeah . . .

JASMINEROSE: So I guess that's just like a game thing for you. Talking to a bunch of different women from behind a screen.

JAMARVELOUS83: A game . . . ?

JASMINEROSE: Like you're not really REALLY interested in meeting someone on here. As in, physically meeting. You just want to be safe and free of intimacy.

JAMARVELOUS83: I've gotta say . . . that last word you just used there is a real boner deflator

JASMINEROSE: Excuse me?

JAMARVELOUS83: :-/ Sorry was trying to make you laugh

JASMINEROSE: Okay

JAMARVELOUS83: I believe a wise woman once said, "This is so intense for a first convo" . . .

JASMINEROSE: Wow.

JAMARVELOUS83: :-/

JAMARVELOUS83: Sorry, you were just talking some heavy stuff there and yeah. I'm just trying to get to know you. Let's go back to Wichita!

JASMINEROSE: No you're not but that's cool.

JAMARVELOUS83: Wasn't I?

JAMARVELOUS83: :-/

JAMARVELOUS83: Jasmine?

JAMARVELOUS83: Rose?

JAMARVELOUS83: Jasrose? Romine?

<JasmineRose has left the chat.>
<JasmineRose is offline.>

<You are now logged out of OkCupid.>

66

NEW TAB:

Google: Jasmine Rose Wichita

11,200,000 results found

NEW TAB:

Grubhub.com

China House Restaurant

Order for delivery: 1 sweet-and-sour chicken, 1 chicken dump-
lings, 1 egg-drop soup, 1 chow fun

Expected arrival time: 45 minutes

NEW TAB:

Google: Empire Wine & Spirit

Order for delivery: 1 12-pack Pacífico, 1 bottle Jack Daniel's

Expected arrival time: 30 minutes

CLOSE TAB. NEW TAB:

MLB.com

Article: The Most Overrated in MLB History?

POST COMMENT:

Um two words, DodgersFan1962: Julio. Teheran. Are we forgetting
#2015Gate?! His 4.04 ERA and 1.31 WHIP?? This guy is nothing
more than a good starter. The end.

FACEBOOK POP-UP NOTIFICATION:

Geraldine Sands invited you to her event:

A Hudson Healing: Ashtanga Yoga Power Prayer for our African
American friends!

Shift + Command + 3

LAUNCH IMESSAGE:

Compose new message to Jen Sands:

Please look at this screenshot of Mom's yoga retreat. Kill me.

GMAIL POP-UP NOTIFICATIONS:

Alexandra Hughes: Status for biocomplex nutritionals?

Forbes: Jamar, renew your subscription to *Forbes* today
and save 30%

Amazon: Your Amazon.com order has shipped!

IMESSAGE POP-UP NOTIFICATION:

JEN SANDS: We need to change our last names.

JAMAR SANDS: lol

JAMAR SANDS: Like, how can I explain it to her

JEN SANDS: Don't even try. I mean, she has BLACK CHILDREN
and she still says "Mama-san"

JAMAR SANDS: Please don't remind me of that dinner at P.F.
Chang's

JEN SANDS: brb at work

JAMAR SANDS: Cool

LAUNCH SPOTIFY:

Search: Eagles > Albums > *The Very Best of the Eagles*

GMAIL POP-UP NOTIFICATION:

Grubhub: Jamar, your Grubhub order is in the works!

SWITCH TO CHROME > MLB.COM TAB:

Article: Legends of MLB, Past, Present, and Future

POST COMMENT:

Sammy Sosa, you fucking assholes. Sammy. Fucking. Sosa. I dare someone to disagree with me. Come on. Bring it.

Refresh.

Refresh.

NEW TAB:

timesunion.com > News

Article: Drought Extends Grip on Upstate New York

Article: Tired of Living Alone? Here's How to Thrive with a Happier Life

Article: Controversial Internet Personality Sebastian White Compares Trans Military Members to Cockroaches

NEW TAB:

Google: Sebastian White + alt-right

RETURN TO MLB.COM TAB.

Refresh.

Refresh.

Refresh.

Refresh.

Refresh.

Refresh.

Refresh.

Refresh.

Refresh.

RETURN TO TIMESUNION.COM TAB.

Article: Teen Charged After Berkshire Farm Fight

Article: Road Closures Planned in Downtown Albany

Article: 2017 Brings a New Year of Resolutions for the State of New York

Article: Six Months Later, Two Violent Sexual Assault Cases Remain Unsolved

FACEBOOK POP-UP NOTIFICATION:

Maria Lockhead likes your post.

GMAIL POP-UP NOTIFICATION:

Grubhub: Jamar, your Grubhub order is on its way!

RETURN TO GOOGLE TAB:

Google: Donald Ellis + Watertown New York + assault

Google: Pear O'Sullivan + Springfield Massachusetts + assault www.timesunion.com/local/Second-Man-Violently-Attacked-By-An-Unidentified-Woman-Baffles-Local-Law-Enforcement-3735483.php

Google: Detective Myles Whirloch + upstate New York

FACEBOOK POP-UP NOTIFICATION:

Jake Pizzalotto tagged you in a photo.

Open Facebook tab.

Photo caption:

Kettlebells with the SandsMan! Best way to Saturday it up.

POST COMMENT:

Now THAT'S how a strict press should look. Good form, homie. See you next Sat.

RETURN TO SPOTIFY:
Search: Kanye West

NEW TAB:
yahoo.com/news
Article: The Best Places to Vacation in the World
Google: Photos of Bali
Google: Photos of family vacations in Bali
Google: Celebrity photos in Bali
Ariticle: Ryan Gosling's Amazing Beach Body
Article: Five Things You Didn't Know About Ryan Gosling
Google: Ryan Gosling official website
Google: Best actor websites + design
Google: Acting classes + Albany New York
Google: Photo studio + headshots + Albany New York
Google: Famous actors actresses born in Albany New York
Google: Megyn Kelly official website
Google: Megyn Kelly pictures + bikini

NEW TAB:
youporn.com

FACEBOOK POP-UP NOTIFICATION:
Jake Pizzalotto likes your comment.

RETURN TO YOUPORN.COM TAB:
Search: Blondes
Video: Bad Little Swedish Fish

IMESSAGE POP-UP NOTIFICATION:

MOM: Hey you! Call Mom when the spirit moves you! You are missed! <prayer emoji> <kisses emoji> <downward dog emoji> <laugh cry emoji>

iMessage > Preferences > Accounts > Disable notifications for this account

Command + Q

Close youporn.com tab.

Close all tabs.

Quit Chrome.

Apple > Sleep

TWO

Username:
Password:

APPLE NOTIFICATION:
Welcome back, Jamar Sands!
Launch Chrome.

NEW TAB:
Google: How to get Hoisin sauce out of a shirt
Google: Dry cleaning pickup service + Albany

GMAIL POP-UP NOTIFICATIONS:
GNC: Get 20% off organic protein powder for the fighter in you
ESPN: Steve Zabrinski accepted your trade.
MLB.com: Order your Chrome Baseball Refractors before February 2017 and save!

RETURN TO GMAIL:
Gmail > Google Calendar > Janaury 7, 2017 reminder >
Grandma's B-day

LAUNCH IMESSAGE:

Compose new message to Jen Sands:

Shit! It's MawMaw's bday today and I totally forgot. Sending her flowers. Will put from both of us.

RETURN TO CHROME:

Google: Flower delivery + Hartford CT

houseofflora.com

Order: 1 Teleflora's Golden Laughter Bouquet

ADD CARD:

MawMaw—Happy ninety-first birthday. You've inspired us our whole lives. I hope you get to eat an entire quiche today and make Mr. Torres cry again during gin rummy, you ruthless poker face! Love you. Your bugs, Jamar and Jen

CLOSE TAB.

Launch Adobe Illustrator.

Launch Snagit.

Launch Coda.

Launch Spotify:

Search: Kid Rock radio

Desktop > Work > Active Projects > Biocomplex Nutritionals

GMAIL POP-UP NOTIFICATION:

House of Flora: Thank you for ordering from House of Flora!

OKCUPID POP-UP NOTIFICATION:

JaMarvelous83, you have a new chat-request message from

Maude.

NEW TAB:

OkCupid.com

Open chat-request message:

MAUDE: Hi Jamar.

MAUDE: Looking for a strong mind to haunt.

MAUDE: I like your walls.

MAUDE: Can I walk through them?

<Accept chat request.>

<You are now chatting with Maude.>

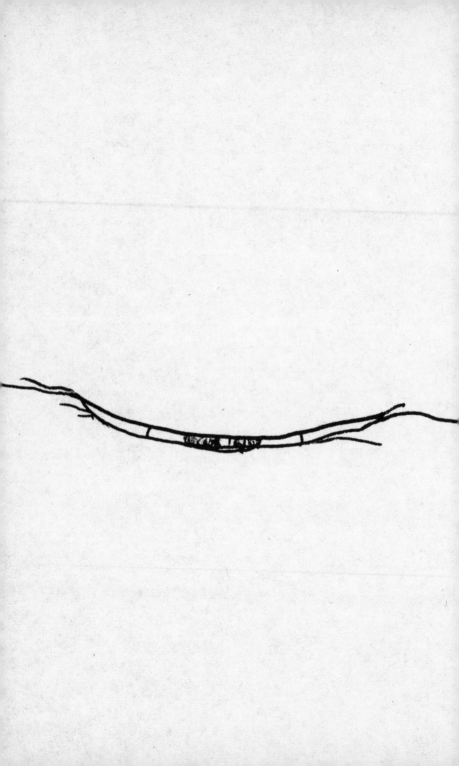

May 8th, 2016

Dear Mr. Ellis,

My name is Marsha Broscov, and I'm a producer of The Melissa Hope Show on BCN (P2+ = 2.1 million viewers). As you may know, Melissa is a legal commentator with the #1 current affairs talk show in the country. We think you are absolutely riveting and have been following your story since your assault a few months ago. We are such big fans! We'd love to bring you on the show to discuss your activism and your thoughts on your attacker.

We'd love to have you on Melissa's show this Friday at 7 p.m. We would provide a car service to and from your residence, a hotel, and hair and makeup at the studio. Let us know your thoughts and looking forward!

Best,
Marsha

May 9th, 2016

Hi Marsha,

Thank you for reaching out. I haven't really done anything of this measure before and I'm not sure I'm entirely comfortable going on a talk show at this time. I don't know. It's still hard for me to speak about it. I'd need to discuss it with my wife. I really don't want to go into the details of what happened that night, that's the main thing for me. I'd rather discuss the culture surrounding sexual assault and how few men report being sexually assaulted, but also how few women are actually believed. That's what I'd rather talk about. Let me know what you think.

Also, hair and makeup wouldn't be necessary. Do guys normally do that?

Thanks,
Donald

P.S. Out of curiosity, how did you get my email address?

May 9th, 2016

Great to hear back from you, Donald!

Why don't we just go ahead and confirm your participation, and you can always pull out if you need to. (Hehe, no pun intended!) I find with these sorts of things, it's always better to get it on the books, then decide. We will of course understand if you change your mind!

Yes, we can absolutely discuss the broader theme of society's role in rape culture and the issues facing men and women today.

Would this Friday, May 13th, work for your scheduled appearance? We can send a car at 2 p.m. for pick up. May I have your address to schedule the car service?

Regarding your email address, we called your daughter's school and someone there gave it to us. Hope that's okay!

Best,
Marsha

HAPPY DAY AFTER OPENING DAY, MY FELLOW BASEBALL PER-
verts! Sorry, inappropriate introduction for group
therapy, I know. Hello, my name is Pear. O'Sullivan. From Massachusetts, proud home of racists
and Red Sox. I've been coming here to Albany Crisis Center
for a while now, as most of you know. Hard to get an old shit-
flower like me to come talk in a room full of—Jesus, what the
hell are you guys again, supermodels for the oil rig industry?
I've never seen such a bunch of handsome, tan lumberjacks.
Anyway, yeah. Here I am. I see there are a few new folks here
today—hey, guys—so I'll sort of reintroduce myself, but I
won't recount the whole thing of it, why I'm here or whatever,
again. You've got my name, but here's a little about me. I'm a
sixty-four-year-old man who's spent his life rejecting any iota

of income to pursue a long and insufferable life of regional stand-up comedy. That's a direct quote from my ex-wife. My third one. I was born in New Mexico and moved to Boston when I was twenty-five. Not for comedy but for a girl. Then I had my heart broken. Not by the girl. By comedy. For various reasons I found myself near here, in Springfield, Mass., which is maybe the worst place for a stand-up to live, but that's how my fucking cards fell. Plus I'm a pussy for the fall foliage. A soft doodle and so forth.

"Ya know . . . the way I see it, what happened to me—why I'm here—I see it as a beautifully executed joke, half a century too late. Knock knock. Who's there? A lady. A lady who? A lady who rapes! You know the rest. I can't believe I was given a lifetime's worth of material at the end of my lifetime. I mean, seriously, why couldn't she've attacked me before I hit sixty, before I got carcinoma of the goiter and a full closet full of shit-stained boxers? Back when I had stamina and good stage presence? Back before I could get senior-citizen discounts at Yankee Candle? She really could've made me a star if she'd taken a second and thought about doing all of this forty years ago, man. Rapists these days: no consideration for the little guy!

". . . Okay, okay, easy on the jokes, Pear, I know, I know. Share your truth, Pear. Speak from the heart, Pear. I know. Listen . . . I started coming to ACC back in August of last year, a few months after my assault. By a woman. A woman they're calling Maude. I gotta laugh when I say that, because it's funny, ya know? It's so awful it's funny. It's nuts! When I first started coming here eight months ago, I didn't talk much. I didn't talk at all. I'd always known I had a life's worth of bad

luck: Raised by a shitty father. Divorced three times, none of which I wanted. A savings account that resembled a relationship between Wells Fargo and Ike Turner. But to be here in my sixties, resting on the very few laurels I've earned in my old age, and have this happen to me? I mean, Jesus. Jesus. Gotta laugh.

"I stopped going onstage, man. I stopped doing a lotta things I loved for a while. Like keeping a journal. Something I've done since I was a kid. How I store all my jokes and thoughts 'n' crap like that. I only started writing again about a month ago. But I stopped for a long time. Also gardening. I used to do that daily, man. Daily. Don't much anymore. Good thing I have a lot of succulents. They're the only things that survived the past months of me sitting in an Adirondack in my backyard, holding a gardening hose in my hand and fantasizing about swinging my neck eternal from the nearest birch. Tree, whatever, you know what I mean. Lucky for me, or those trees, I couldn't find one of them I'd want to put through that. My death, I mean. I believe a man's gotta have an understanding with the tree he's going to hang himself from. I do. A relationship. It's one thing to hang yourself from a piece of metal in the garage, or ceiling plaster, but a living fucking tree? They're sacred. *Sacred.* They're the longest-living organisms on Earth. They can live off air alone. They can't die from old age, only diseases and lightning 'n' shit. I mean, they fucking talk to each other! Like, willow trees, man. They warn each other about bacteria with this shit called phenols. It's true! They heal people just by being looked at. That's a fact. That's why they're planted outside hospitals so sick people can look at 'em. Trees are powerful, man, trees are just powerful. So you

can't just climb up there and tie your neck from one and call it
a Wednesday. No. A man's gotta have an understanding with
that tree, if he's going to do that.

"Okay, listen, my time's almost up. Thanks for listening to me
today. I guess I want to say . . . I want to say to the new guys
here, look, it's okay to process your shit however you want
to. It's your shit. It's no one else's shit. As long as you're not
hurting someone else. Your hell is yours and you get to decide,
okay? You get to decide when you're ready. It's important that
I say this, though: It's not your fault, whatever happened to
you. It's not your fault. But healing your own pain does belong
to you now. When we become aware, we become responsible.
Also, Pamela from registration makes the best Goddamn waffles I've ever had and she sets up a waffle table over there after
group every week. Live a little."

TWO

APRIL 3, 2017

Today there were some new guys that came to group. Three of them. One of them's got a face I'd know anywhere. Jamar. Jamar with the bronze circles swallowing his eyes. Jamar with the skin he hasn't washed in weeks and the black hair painted on his scalp. Jamar with the backward baseball cap that sits on a head no longer connected to its rail-thin body, a body that looks like it's been starved for months. My little brother in shame. In anger. He's like me, like the bud of a moonflower. Poor fucking moonflower bud. I didn't even have to hear his last name to know who he is. My abused successor. The kid I read about from Albany. The kid who was attacked back in January. I know there's not many options for support groups in these re-

gions, especially just for guys, so it's not surprising he'd end up here, alongside me, broken and life-fucked. It's strange to know I share this story with someone else. That I share her ghost with another man. That I'll be in the same room, weekly, with him. To know he knows what I know. Her small, cold, heavy hands. The smell of her skin, like pewter and rotting potting soil. Awful. The feeling of her long, hair dragging like a rake. The sound of her crawling toward me. Not on all fours but all four hundreds, like a stampede of millipedes. Like a multi-animal.

APRIL 4

Idea for sketch: Men who high-five but have ~~shrunken hands~~ enlarged fingers? Both?

Joke idea: Flatulent high heels for girl clowns (Remember woman in parking lot at Walmart)

Call Jim back, set up set at the Sour Milk for Dec

~~An app to find the best apps?~~ stupid

APRIL 5

I had a dream I was onstage and I opened with a joke about a measles outbreak at a strip club. I kept telling the joke over and over again. Same joke. Same exact words and punch. Each time I'd change inflection, add sounds, change emphasis on certain words, but always the exact same words in the joke. Audience laughed every single time, the same way. Was pissing me off. Wanted them to get that the joke was that I was telling the same joke too many times, not the joke itself, which is fuck-

ing dumb. Hat-on-a-hat-type deal. They didn't get. Was stuck in loop. Was tired of saying the joke. Started to break down. They found this even funnier. Joke on me.

APRIL 6

Called Whirloch today. Haven't spoken in four months. Since I flipped out and hung up on him. Shot the messenger as it were. He didn't deserve all that. I'm sure he's used to it though, in cases where they can't find suspects. I like Myles, I do. He's got an Elmer Fudd quality about him. He's even got a funny little hat like Fudd. And he's a little fatty, like me. I don't hate the guy. I hate the inefficient fucksacks at the DA and Myles's superiors. I blame THEM for letting more of these attacks happen. For fucking up evidence or whatever lazy work's been going on. It's been more than a fucking YEAR and, so far, three of us have been assaulted and they've gotten NO-WHERE. Nothing! Anyway, I called. Told him Jamar's been coming to ACC. Jamar the poor little flower bud.

I also just wanted to get an update on the investigation. He said it's good to hear from me. There's still very little to go on but they're doing everything they can. Can't discuss Bud's case with me either, other than to say they are tracking down some IP info. I say what's IP info and he says it's a way for them to see where she chatted with him from. Like a license plate for a computer. Maybe that will give them some more leads. "More leads." Seems crazy to me, considering her fucking body was all over mine and probably Bud's too. They did find one hair though. One extremely long white hair. Six feet long. No matches though, so that was that. She's been jumping from city to city, no pattern. I ask if there's anything I can do and he says

not really, which I know is the truth but it still lights up my anxiety like a black guy at David Duke's birthday party. How can they not find this fucking monster? This pigmentless cunt? No eyewitnesses. No fingerprints. He asks me to watch out for Bud and maybe try to get him to talk more. I tell him I'll try.

I ask Whirloch if he can tell me if Bud's attack was worse than mine, just so I know what I'm dealing with. All he says is yes, in some ways it was worse.

APRIL 6

Maude. Ugly Maude. Hideous, revolting, slob Maude. Fat dumb bitch Maude, with cankles and demon egg sacks growing in her gums. Hooved Maude. Fingerless piss sucker with a hive of pussies between her thighs. Maude who crawls around like a freak. A repulsive piece of shit of a woman. Ann Coulter with the face of Ann Coulter without makeup on. Cher with typhoid. Like a fucking burn victim with babies' decapitated fingers for eyelashes. With breath like rotting fish and a trail of fur running up the backs of her legs and two giant claws for tits. I'll bet she only eats wasps and sleeps on a mattress filled with a thousand scalped dick skins. Princess and the fucking PEAnis Maude. Come over again, you queen of dog pus. Where are you where are you where the hell are you? Come over again, you harpy coward. You daughter of an infection. Where are you, you cloaked crone? Where the fuck are you Maude what are you

APRIL 10

Bud sat across from me today and just listened in group,

like he's done every Monday. Quiet. Passed on talking. I did the same. Wasn't feeling like sharing. Some weeks are worse than others. Some weeks I can stand on my own two feet. Some weeks I am reborn without legs. Like getting out of bed and standing was never even in my repitoir. Repitour? Fuck it I don't know how you spell that. In group I listened to Bobby talk about anger. It was really moving. He quoted this guy Krishnamarty who said, "Anger has that peculiar quality of isolation; like sorrow, it cuts one off, and for the time being, at least, all relationship comes to an end. Anger has the temporary strength and vitality of the isolated. There is a strange despair in anger; for isolation is despair." (I asked him to read it to me again after group and I copied it down word for word.)

I know despair. Known it for years. I've introduced it to my family and spent holidays with it. I argue with it about how to load the dishwasher. I watch TV with it at night. I take a shit in the morning by its side. I go for long walks at dusk and let it spew its foul thoughts in my ears. I take it to the doctor when it's not feeling well. I ride home with it after every show I do, especially the good ones. That's when despair really likes to be there for me. To remind me it was just a fluke. I thank despair for keeping me honest. For never lying to me. I take it up to my place for a nightcap. I fuck it to feel better. I wake up a bitter man.

Bud was at the waffle table after group so I went up. What the hell do I have to lose. Just a coupla rapeys hangin' round the flavored-syrup bar! No baseball cap this time, but a Red Sox jersey. Number 24. I know that number. Told him how I'd lived in Boston for a while. Told him Price is my favorite player too. Ask if he knows the Dwight Evans story. He says he doesn't. I tell him how the Sox retired the jersey, which

was Dwight Evans's . . . until Price came along. Price wanted Dewey's number and Dewey said he'd only give his blessing on one condition: Price had to beat his record in home runs. Bud smiled and liked the story. I ask if he's ever seen the Sox play, he says no. I tell him they're the best and if he's gonna see them he's got to see them in Fenway Park. Where they're from. It's the best stadium out there. That stadium is the heart in the whole body of baseball. He says thanks and we shake hands like regular guys. Like no particular men.

APRIL 11

KrishnaMURTI not MARTY idiot

Order Krishnamurti book on anger

Order fertilizer

Gotta stop drinking coffee too much heartburn

New Latin words I'd like to coin:

Oligarchery: A fun new game for dictators

Dichotautonomy: Easy word for separation of church and state!

Emeritolstoy: Never having to read that asshole again

~~Alibisexual~~ dumb

~~Cum Laude Latte~~ Also dumb

Antibelluminosity: The glorification of war-destroyed cities for the sake of tourism

Carpe per diem: Give me my fucking money or else

~~Monolilithfair~~ terrible

Christ these are all puns

APRIL 11

I just looked up a bunch of articles about Bud. I wasn't sure I'd want to do that but I'm glad I did. Myles said in some ways his was worse but from what I can read there's no way that's true. Sounds like the guy just had a bad and bizarre night of screwing. Jamar talked to her over three different sessions on a dating site. On a live chat-type deal. They set up a time to finally meet but she said she could just come over to his place instead and they could hang there. What guy's gonna say no to that? She came over with a wolf mask on. What the Mother Teresa actual fuck? She gave him one too. Some kind of role-playing thing maybe. They got drunk. She had all the lights off and they started going at it on his couch. He told Whirloch she bit him and he didn't like that so he tried to stop her but she told him to shut up and just enjoy it. What guy's gonna say no to that? So he let her keep going even though he wanted her to stop. After they finished he fell asleep for a few minutes and when he woke up she was gone. He was still in the dark. When he turned the lights on he saw blood everywhere. A lot of it, all over his crotch. All over his couch and floor. A trail leading to the front door. But he wasn't in any pain. So it had to be hers, I'm guessing?

It also says the bite marks were not made by human teeth. I need a drink.

APRIL 12

Dreamed my mother was trying to breastfeed a lion cub. It was half lion, half prehistoric . . . thing. With scales on its lips. I knew I had to kill it before it killed her. She didn't understand

what it would grow up to be. I wanted to protect her from it. Just a terrible dream. It said my name as it died. Ma screamed.

APRIL 15

Sox got a game coming up at Fenway against the Yankees. I fucking hate the Yankees. They have a brand of cologne, for fuck's sake. They're a bunch of chauvinist dopers. Anyway, got two tickets. Thinking of inviting Bud. Don't know yet. Maybe.

APRIL 17

Today in group I decided to try out some new material. Thought that could be two-birds-one-stone-type situation: test material while also engaging in group. (Bevypetrum? Latin for a bunch of birds and a rock? Maybe. Least it's not a pun.)

Bud didn't show today. Hope the kid's all right.

APRIL 17

Just woke up it's 3:15 a.m. couldn't sleep wanted a snack so I went to the kitchen and a red light was blinking on Coral which was weird because I never heard the phone ring once while I was sleeping so how could there be a new message? Played it and it was like some weird noise. Some animal giving birth or something, some low howling. Maybe a messed-up phone frequency.

Wait. No.
Crying. Like a man crying.

APRIL 18

Didn't sleep much. Talked to Myles. Apparently the FBI's got its dick in the investigation now. Jesus. I ask if it's that serious and he says yeah pretty much. He asks how I'm holding up. I say fine. He asks about Bud. I tell him he didn't come in yesterday. I say I read about Bud's assault and it didn't seem worse than mine by even a long shot so I wasn't sure why I was the one to be doing all the reaching out. Myles sighed that big fat man wheeze of his and said, off the record, did you read about all that blood we found? I say yeah, the bitch's blood. He says no. It belonged to an animal. A dead animal they found in the hallway. A cat.

I'm gonna puke.

I don't understand, I tell him. She poured dead cat blood all over him? No he says.

I say I still don't understand. He says yes you do.

Let's just say we found bodily fluid—Jamar's—in the deceased animal.

God

Fuck

APRIL 19

Didn't sleep last night. Not hungry this morning. Want a cigarette. And a Scotch. What Ayn Rand I wouldn't read for a Scotch. I've been sober for almost a year, and I'm thinking of breaking today. Thinking about moving also. Going back to Santa Fe. But first I'm going to Home Depot to buy new locks. I'm gonna add more locks to the front and back door. A padlock at least, for each. And bars on the windows. That will take a little time but I'll find a company to do it. Also, a gun. Gonna get a gun today.

APRIL 19

Was at Home Depot getting locks when I saw a bunch of young sweetbays in Gardening. Didn't even know they were in bloom yet! And not just any magnolias but light blue ones, which is something I've never seen before. Only ever seen the white and pink. But blue! Like a faded teal color almost. Cheered me up. Little blue fuckers. I grabbed a couple and some supplies and came back here and started mulching. The whole day got away from me.

So get this: When I got home Coral had two messages for me. One was from a collection asshole but the other one— get this—the other one was from a guy named Donald Ellis. Yeah, that Donald Ellis. The dad guy they found behind a dumpster. He said he got my number from the phone book. I didn't even know those things existed anymore. He wanted to know if I wanted to come to some march he's holding. A vigil for survivors of sexual assault. Survivors? I thought we were victims.

They're meeting in Albany I guess. I don't know about all that.

Did I ever tell you why I call her "Coral"? It's short for Coral Reef. I call her that because she's ancient, practically extinct, and human beings shit all over her. (Now that they have super cool cell phones! Who needs a landline!)

Plus, she has a name because it's just nice to have someone in the house to say hello and goodbye to.

APRIL 20

Looked up info on missing pets in Albany. Cats, in specific. Not that many.

Lots of cockatiels for some reason.

APRIL 21

Joke idea: What regular guys use to jack off with compared to what schizo-rapists use to jack off with. Socks compared to fresh roadkill.

Nope.

APRIL 24

Bud was back today. For the first time, he talked during group. Mostly just about work and family. He makes websites for a living. Talked about his hovering white hippie mom and low-key black dad who works for the Department of Motor Vehicles. Says his sister has been really great through every-thing that happened. Wish I had had a family member like that. His sister is the reason he came to ACC. Then Bud tells everyone why he's there, what I'd known all along. Not any

details, just that he was one of Maude's victims and didn't want
to talk about it, just wanted to get it out in the open. All the
guys gave supportive grunts and nodded their heads. A bunch
of eyes turned toward me, of course. How could they not? Bud
kept his on the ground when he spoke. After group he came up
to me at the waffle table. Kind of a nice surprise. He told me
he read about the Evans story but I got part of it wrong. Evans
didn't tell Price he had to beat his record if he wanted number
24, he just had to win a World Series. Look at this little shit,
correcting me! Love it. I tell him about the Sox game in a couple
weeks and how I got tickets if he wants to go. Boston's only a
couple hours drive from here. He says thanks but no, he's not
going out these days. I say I understand completely, believe
me. I felt like a moron and stood there silent for half a second,
which felt like half a decade, before I took my banana-nut waffles and pissed off.

APRIL 24

Left ACC and couldn't quite shake a feeling. I was driving
home with the Replacements on full blast but still something
wasn't right. Chris Mars' drums on "Kiss Me on the Bus"
were kicking harder than usual, harder than a herd of hyena
hearts. Or a bevy or whatever the hell those things are called.
Something's not right, I'm thinking. The drums. The drums
aren't right. There's too much bass drum, too many feet on that
one little pedal. Or extra pedals or something, I don't know. I
turned it up louder and listened. Not right. Then the rhythm
wasn't right either. Not even on tempo. That's when I turned
it down and realized the sound wasn't in the song but coming
from my car. From the trunk. Something was pounding on the

trunk from inside. *Who's in my fucking trunk? Should I pull over? Should I wait to check when I get home?* Thought about the new gun I have at home and decided to get it first, then pop the trunk. I parked in my driveway and loaded up the pistol. I'm so fucking clumsy with bullets, they just aren't for me. I'm all mouth and no murder.

Who's in there, I yelled. Tell me your name. *Bang. Bang. Bang.*

No answer. I cocked the pistol, unlocked the trunk, aimed, and stepped back. But it was just a bird. A crow. It flew out and into the trees. Heart was pounding. *How did a crow get in my fucking trunk?* Figured I must've left it open when I came back from Home Depot.

I went to shut the trunk and inside I saw . . . birds. Dead ones. Dozens of them.

Different kinds of dead birds everywhere.

APRIL 24

Didn't feel like being alone tonight so I picked up some company and brought her home. She and me and despair go way back. I got the most expensive one I could afford. The more expensive, the better she'll treat you. I brought her into the house and showed her around the place. Not much to show. The collection of awful racist coffee mugs I've acquired across the country over the years. My library of books: mostly botany-related and memoirs from kings like Carlin and Martin. I prefer memoirs to biographies because there's no fun in reading crusty academic writing about the life of, say, Bill Hicks. Who wants to read that? I don't want to hear about the '91 Relent-

less tour from some guy who wasn't there or even some guy who was there. I want to hear about it from the guy who WAS the '91 Relentless tour. Hicks didn't write a memoir, but still. I'd rather listen to his albums than read a soulless trough of assumptive sentences on the man.

I showed her my collection of Andy Kaufmans. Bobble-heads. Ugly misshapen Kaufman knit patchwork dolls. Bizarre fan figurines of Kaufman with lima beans for eyes. All in Andy's image. I've found the weirdest shit over the years. Some guy made a statue of him out of glued-together hot sauces. Wasn't going to buy that and have it shipped from Tennessee though. A lady in Arizona had a swimming-pool float of his face. All kinds of things Andy probably would've fucking hated. Or maybe loved. Hard to say.

I took her into the kitchen and pulled out two glasses. Helped her out of her brown wrap and tossed it on the floor. Told her to make herself comfortable. She insisted on sitting on the kitchen counter. That made me happy. I told her I was pretty fucking down today. Told her how I'd been to group and talked to Bud. How I came home to my handsome blue magnolias blooming away in the front yard, shitting leaves all over the place. About finally getting invited to do a showcase for Jimmy Fallon's people. But something was still missing. There's a cave in me. A hardened opening I don't want and don't know how to close. She sat there listening, looking beautiful. Felt good to be listened to like that. No judgment. Then she said one word. "Dynamite." What about dynamite, I asked and moved closer. She whispered, that's how you get rid of a cave you don't want. I smiled. You want to be my dynamite, baby, I said and put my arms around her. I delicately took off her plastic and unscrewed

her head, then I poured her legs into my glass and drank her
until I could feel the fuse ignite.

So drunk. Drunky drunk fuck my funk im up im up!
My name is maudy potty pussy mouth monster. I wear
dresses
and have a huundred thumbtacks for kneecaps.
I'll squirm across your stomac and puncture your organs
like water balloons.
I will fuuuuuck your death hole into a coffined mind.
I am 25 yers old have a long face like two horse heads sewn
together
and hair that drags a mile long behind me.
Ha!!! One long fucking hair they found! Six feet of shferwww
Fuck you I can spell wasted

I am maudeyy and I am 38 years old and want to come into
your house
and break
your fingers with my husked wings.
No one knows how fucking old I am! I could be a vampire!!!!
I am 41 and covered in bear shit and lipstick
and talk with a mouth full of breeding mice.
I'm fiftyfuck years old and hate men
like I hate showers
like I hate fingernail files
like I hate sports
and sex and guys named peary bear.
I'm 85 years old and I am a wrinkled spawn.
I am the illiterate clitoris of a temptress.

Take that sentence and shove it up your pee hole, Poe!
Who's the fucking poet now you raven licker

My name is maude
and I have one eye and one slug to look with
and I have one lip and one piece of mold to kiss with
and I have one ear and one dead bat to hear from
and I have one hand and one squid tentacle to hold you
my name is maude and I'll rape all the little boys I want to,
thank you.

I have a gun, pretty bird
I have a gun now
come and get me you ghost rot
come and try me you fuck shit

I will sneak up on you in churches! At your daddy's! When
you sleep! Water your lawn little cowboy no one's watching. Not
Maudy no! I'm nowhere and everywhere all at the same time.

I'm fucking nowhere
right behind you

THREE

MAY 1

Haven't written in a while. On purpose. Wasn't going to. Been angry with myself since last week. More than angry. Despondent. A year of sobriety flushed down the shitter. Went back and read my drunk writing. Jesus Christ. Made me laugh but also broke my fucking heart. You can't live like this, Pear. Jumping in and out of your own grave. Wasn't planning on writing or gardening for a long time, as punishment. But today Bud came up before group and asked if I was okay. He actually asked ME that. I guess I looked like shit. I told him I was fine. Just, dealing. He said he'd like to try and go to the game this week with me if I still have a ticket for him. I do.

MAY 1

Left a message for that Donald guy. Called him back. I missed his thing, his vigil thing in Albany, but it's polite to call someone back when they've reached out like that. Call it part of my New Life Resolutions.

Magnolias maintained themselves nicely even while covered in my inebriated urine for the last week, which I only just discovered they'd been drenched in.

MAY 3
Pear's New Life Resolutions
1. *No drinking* under any circumstances. *Consider AA if you have to.*
2. *Go for a walk every day.*
3. *Eat less meat.*
4. *Call and check in with Mom more.*
5. *Meditation?*
6. *Get out bronze-age comics—Zap, Cerebus, etc. (connect with fun kid stuff)*
7. *Go on a date. Maybe.*
8. *Do 10 push-ups every morning.*
9. *Fix the stuff broken while drunk: shed door, back patio window, recliner chair, back scratcher, left shoe.*

MAY 6
What a game! Sox won in the bottom of the 9th. Tied up in the 8th with bases loaded every glorious second. Couldn't have asked for a better first game for a Sox fan like Bud to see. We met at Island Creek Oyster Bar first as he mentioned he's never had an oyster before and I told him I believed it was a Massachusetts state felony to enter Fenway a mollusk-less man. Watching someone eat an oyster for the first time is one of the best things you can ever witness. The kid covered it in every sauce they could possibly provide, then plucked it out of its juices, shook it off, put it on his plate, and CUT IT IN HALF

WITH A FORK AND KNIFE. It was the best Goddamned
thing I'd ever seen in my entire life. Horrifying. Granted they
were Pacific oysters the size of a shoe but Jesus a fork and a
knife?? I am still laughing right now and it's almost midnight.
I showed him how to just suck the little fucker down, juices and
all. Still he sorta nibbled at the edge of the shell and shook the
thing toward his mouth. Also he asked for a side of tartar sauce.
I interrupted that request immediately. That will get you killed
around here, I said.

After the game I drove back to Springfield and listened to
Monty Python's "Matching Tie and Handkerchief," then the
Who's "Tommy" of course, then Costello's "Pretty Words" over
and over until I got to my exit, switched off the stereo, and just
listened to the distant farts of an incoming thunderstorm.

MAY 7
Such a great week, then I get a call from Bobby from group
who tells me I better go get the Dispatch, *as in the* Dispatch
fucking national newspaper, so I do and there on the second
fucking page is the headline "Details on a String of Violent
Sexual Assaults Rocking the Northeast," with a large picture
of none other than Jamar Sands. These fucking kweef keepers.
Putting a picture of THE VICTIM in the paper, like a prom
portrait or an actor's headshot. Blood is boiling right now.
Someone leaked everything to them. Everything. They tell about
the dead cat and the blood. The article talks about my case and
Donald Ellis, who's doing some radio interviews now in an
effort to get the public more involved. They don't give details on
our cases but FULL details on Jamar's. Full details on state-

ments he gave to the police, including that he pissed himself when he saw all the blood. I know Myles didn't do this. Myles would never do this.

I phoned him up and blew a shotgun of words through his ear. He let me scream for 10 minutes. Who the fuck DID this, I ask. He says he's as angry as me, that I should believe him, because this compromises the cases in many ways. They're looking into whoever leaked the information. I say, do you know how fragile Jamar is? Do you have any idea what shape we're in out here? When we hang up I feel such useless rage, such directionless blame. I call Bud but he doesn't answer. I tell him to call me. He doesn't fucking call. I don't know what to do. I tell him to please show up to group tomorrow. No matter what. I tell him I'll be there and I'll buy every fucking Sunday Dispatch in the whole Goddamn state and I'll burn them. I'll burn them all.

MAY 7

Just got off the phone with Donald. I commended him on everything he's been doing publicly. I could never do those things. I could make jokes about doing those things but I could never actually do them.

On the phone he asked me if I'd read the Dispatch story on Bud. Is a duck's dick damp, Donald, of course I have, everyone's fucking read it, it's the Dispatch. He asked me how I was feeling. Honestly, no one has ever asked me that. Not the police. Not the doctors. No one at group. Not Coral. No one. So I didn't really know how to respond. What do you mean how am I feeling, I ask. Are you feeling okay, he says. Is there

anything I can do for you? The questions caught me off guard. I told him I was fine but thanks. Mostly I'm just worried about the kid. I can't get ahold of the kid. He'll surface, Donald says to me. He'll surface and he'll come find you. Because that's all we have, he says. We have each other. No one else knows what we've been through besides us.

You sure you're good, he says. Yeah I'm good, I say. We hang up the phone.

I cry harder than I've ever cried in my entire life. I cry until I evaporate.

FOUR

HI, GOOD MORNING. GOOD TO SEE YOU ALL TODAY. ESPEcially my pal Jamar, who saw his first Sox game last week! Pretty great game, too.

"Jamar, you don't know this, but I've been calling you 'Bud' for some time now, behind your back. A nickname of sorts. 'Bud' as in the bud of a moonflower, which only blooms at night. You and me, Bud, we only grow in the dark now, don't we, brother? So thank you for coming today. I want to share a story that's, ya know, not easy to share. I've never told it to anyone, so, bear with me.

"Couple of months ago, I talked to you guys about trees for a second. How a man had to have an understanding with one if he wanted to take his own life by hanging himself from that tree. So, last year, there was this tree. A tree in the woods

behind my house—a maple—that was very special to me and everyone in town. If you live in or anywhere near Springfield, you've seen her or heard of her. A long time ago she was nick-named Maggie, short for Magnificent. Maggie was very old, much older than the other maples around there, for some rea-son. Really a well-loved and well-lived specimen. The prior owners of my house told me they'd buried three dogs beneath her over two generations. And my neighbor Mrs. Beckett scat-tered her mother's ashes around her. Maggie stood out among the other trees, like she had her own force field or something. Ya know, it's a strange thing to find a maple like that, sur-rounded by a dense population of other maples but with a fifty-foot diameter of ground space surrounding her, like she was her own island. Like a bull's-eye. It gave her the sole glow of the moon at night, and a spotlight of sun all day.

"The most spectacular thing about Maggie was how the other trees treated her. They didn't grow straight up to the sky like most trees, no. They grew at an angle. They grew toward her. All of them, slanted in her direction. I'm not being poetic or nothin', this is real—a guy made a postcard out of a photo he took of that very image. You can buy it at Dougie's Drug-store. Imagine that: a large circle of trees all tilting in toward one bigger tree in the middle of them. In the fall, when all the other leaves turn gold and red and brown, Maggie's would turn pure white. From green to just . . . white. Not silver—not like a cream color, man—but white white, like a hotel towel. Once I saw a strong wind blow through her, and only her, while all the other trees just stood still and watched. She had her own atmosphere, man. She was her own fucking world.

"I was home one night putting notes together for a gig in

Philly when the doorbell rang. I wasn't expecting anyone. No one was there, so I stepped out onto my porch, and something was bagged over my head. I was knocked out cold. It happened like that. In a split second. One minute you're trying to work out the logic for a meta fart joke, the next you're waking up tied to your own radiator. I couldn't see anything other than the print of the fabric covering my face, some blurred blue, which smelled like . . . perfume. Girls' perfume. I'll never, ever forget that fucking smell. Ever. I could hear the person going through drawers in my bedroom. I tried to talk to them. I asked them what they wanted. I told them I have no money, nothing they'd want. I told them I was a comic for a living, for Christ's sakes, I had nothing they'd want, believe me. They came into the room and I felt . . . their tongue run down every fucking notch of my spine, like from the base of my skull all the way down . . . just, all the way down, man. That's what I thought it was—a tongue. All slimy and stiff and just disgusting.

"I need a second, guys.
"Give me a second here.

"They never found any saliva on my back, or anywhere else, for that matter. That's because it wasn't her tongue. It was a broom handle. My own broom, covered in my own God damn lube. I know you know what I'm about to say, but I need to say it out loud anyway, okay? I need to say it out loud because no one here knows it. She sodomized me with that

handle, over and over, as I screamed for help. It's a pain . . . it's a cellular pain now, okay? It's not a memory, it lives in me like a heart. And I will never forget this, all right? I will never forget the sound of her laughing as I screamed for her to stop. My eyes focused in on the only thing they could see: the pattern of tiny cartoon-drawn trees with smiley faces on them and birds flying around.

"It was days before they told me it was a dress she'd tied around my face.

"A fucking dress with a print of little birds and happy trees.

"And the sound . . . that laugh . . . like sped-up thunder. . . . like a whistle in reverse . . . shrill. Like a choir of a thousand fucking mothers. Undeniably female. Undeniably.

"My buddy found me there in my living room, blindfolded, with a dress wrapped around my face and a broomstick still up my ass—Christ, can you imagine what kind of crazy shit he must've thought I was into?—he called the cops immediately. They came and took me to the hospital. I was made to stand in a room and undress on a sterile sheet, in case any fibers or things fell off my body or my clothes. I had to stand there, naked, while they went over every inch of me with their latex gloves on, as if I was a specimen. I was humiliated. I had to lean over and let them take samples from inside me. I had to . . . I had to be examined. I had to let them stick their fingers into the place that was so fucking sore . . . that had just been . . . Listen. This sounds like a joke, doesn't it? This doesn't sound real, does it? I know. I wasn't allowed to take a shower before they did

any of this. I had to stand there with her SMELL still ON ME. They had charts and wrote down everything possible about my horrible body and its condition. They had to do x-rays to make sure nothing was damaged on the inside.

"I was working on a joke about a fart-joke expert and then I was in a hospital getting an x-ray of my rectal lining.

"I came back into my house the next day a changed man. I found it exactly the way I'd left it the day before. My journal still laid out on the table, untouched. The paint scratched off the radiator where I tried to claw through.

"Tell me how a man's supposed to live after something like that?

"Tell me?

"Maggie and her majesty had a different effect on me after that. The sight of her brought no joy. I'd leave group here, all jokes and smiles 'n' shit, head home, drink a liter of Wild Turkey, and walk out into the woods to see her. All she reminded me of was those happy fucking trees on that dress. I started to go see Maggie every night while drunk and piss on her.

"'You know what I would've done to that bitch, if I could've?' I'd say to Maggie. 'I would've broken every inch of her. I would've cut off all her hair and made her choke on it. I would've ripped her apart from her ribs with my bare fucking hands. I would've . . . I would've raped her worse.'

"Maggie never said anything back to me. Gave me no sign

she was listening or cared. I reminded her that it was a member of her own family that had violated me—that broomstick. In my drunk, traumatized mind, she was somehow complicit.

"One night after visiting her, I went home and got my garden hose out of the shed. Remember how I told you I'd only thought about it? I lied. I climbed Maggie and tied the hose from her lowest branch, which was still ten feet off the ground, easy. I tied all the right knots and dropped my sorry ass from her limb. I was ready to die.

"Not three seconds in, the branch broke and I hit the ground, gasping for air. Christ, I was thankful, but also confused. That's a big fucking branch I chose, steady enough for me to stand on the fucking thing and it didn't even bend, so why did it just break off completely like that? Had Maggie done it on purpose? I stared up at her giant elbows and I swear she was staring down at me with pity. I couldn't cry. I was too fucking angry to cry. Why'd she interfere?

"I went back to my house in a drunken rage and into the shed out back. Got my chain saw. Drank some more. Went back and stared her down. I screamed at her to stop looking at me. When she wouldn't, I took the saw to her gut. Even in that state, I could feel the entire forest open its thousands of eyes and gasp. Maggie's leaves fell over me as she trembled, like hands trying to pull me away.

"I WOKE UP THE NEXT MORNING AT HER FOOT. I'D BLACKED OUT right there, the chain saw still stuck in her like a rose in a bullfighter's mouth. I'd only managed to get about halfway through her, that's how big she was. That's how pathetic I

was. I threw up immediately. I couldn't believe what I'd done. I still can't. I wedged the blade out from between her sap-wood, and she creaked in pain. Her blood ran down the side of her trunk. I touched its sugared ooze. I wanted to kill my-self all over again. I wanted to put her out of her misery and finish the job, then run to her falling side and let her crush me to death.

"I'd read somewhere you can dress a tree's wounds just like a human's so I ran home, my head fucking pounding, and grabbed everything I had: hydrogen peroxide, manure compost, a bag of fireplace ashes, and Saran Wrap. I made a kind of makeshift bandage, first cleaning and disinfecting her wound, then packing it with a pastelike mixture of ash and manure. Then I wrapped it up in cellophane.

"That day, I quit drinking. I checked on her daily for weeks. Every day, she looked weaker. I took the cellophane off to let the wound breathe. Bugs attacked it. A couple times, the rain completely washed the dressing out from between her and I had to start all over again. She never fully bloomed over the end of the summer. Her bark grew a strange color and began to dry. I'd take a chair out there and sit next to her and rub oils on her, tell her I was sorry for what I'd done.

"One morning I woke up to a strong wind outside. I had to close all the windows and tie down the tarp over my gar-dening supplies. I was in the kitchen when I heard a roaring sharp snap come from deep in the woods. A family of deer came tearing through the yard, and my windows rattled. A few seconds later, the entire house shook. It sounded like a shuttle reentering the Earth's atmosphere. I knew . . . I knew, right then, Maggie was gone.

"I ran out to find her long body lying in the arms of several trees standing around her. They didn't let her touch the ground. What I'd done . . . What I'd done was murder. Her fresh, fully exposed stump was spitting up sap like some kinda weak fountain. Mrs. Beckett had also heard the sound and came running. When she saw Maggie down, she dropped to her knees and started screaming.

"I'm telling you this story because everyone who loved Maggie and cared for her believed it was the gusts that took her life that day. But it was me. I took her life. I took her life because I thought my life was taken from me. Because I was drunk. Because I was angry. A stupid fucking angry Neanderthal. A weakling. A chicken-shit. I've never admitted I was the one who felled her. Maggie the Magnificent Maple Tree. But I'm admitting it now. Her body still hangs there, suspended in midair in the arms of her family.

"How can you go on living when you're now being lived in? When you've been invaded? How can you tell a joke and enjoy laughter without hearing the one laugh that owns every root in you now? How can you accept air into your lungs from the very perennials whose life you've taken? How can you forgive the person . . . the *woman* who raped you, who has no face to forgive, who has no intention to understand, who is nowhere forever and everywhere inside you for eternity? How can you forgive yourself? How can you enjoy the trees and not plead continuous fucking guilt to them? How can you end your own suffering, without ending completely? How can you accept touch? Or walk through your life, a lived wound, forever avoiding some terrible, inevitable wind."

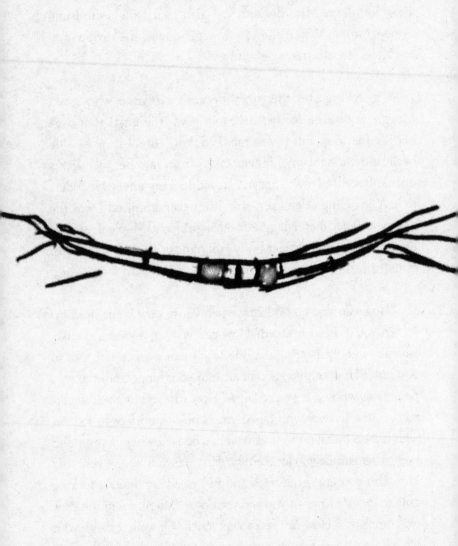

May 15th, 2016

Ms. Broscov,

    I felt compelled to write you after appearing on Friday's segment, as I was extremely upset about what happened. You promised me we would not go over the details of my assault but would instead discuss the broader topic of the culture that surrounds what happened to me. Do you know how it feels to be asked on live television about whether my attacker "grunted" during the assault? Or to insinuate I somehow might've asked for this because I was having drinks at a bar without my wife after work? You might say that's not what Melissa Hope was insinuating, but don't insult my intelligence. And to ask me such deeply personal questions like that, on air, about my children? You promised me you wouldn't do that. And now I'm back where I started, reliving the whole experience. It's all fucked up again. It has taken every bit of strength I have to even get to the point where I could talk about this publicly.

    I should start my own show, if this is the way "journalists" behave. If this is the respect you show survivors.

Donald

May 16th, 2016

Mr. Ellis,

Kindly reread our correspondence. I made no such promise.
I am sorry you had a bad experience but if it's any
consolation, our ratings were fantastic for your segment and I
do believe your appearance, while difficult for you, was for the
greater good and will benefit us all in the long run.

Yours,
Marsha

P.S. You are such a smart guy! A GREAT voice to your
community. Let us know when you've signed a deal. We'll want
an exclusive.

IV

Yeah . . . Yeah hi, this message is for the editor of your publication. Of the Dispatch *national newspaper. My . . . Listen, I'm just wondering, Mr. Editor, I have a question for you. How would you feel? Yeah . . . you, you . . . tell me, since you have all the answers. How . . . how would you feel if this happened to someone you loved and a paper wrote about it in the detail that you did? How . . . you piece of shit . . . I'm . . . I can't—You can't just do these things to people, ya know? We aren't currency. We aren't . . . God, we are trying to LIVE, Morris. Do you know that? My friend Jamar is trying to LIVE, and you just want us DEAD. It's better for your word count if we are brutalized, shamed, humiliated, just . . . just . . . you, you want us under the ground, don't you? How many shovels do you own, you fucking prick? How many . . . how many of our fucking skeletons do you need to dig up?*

Leave us alone, man. Leave Jamar Sands THE FUCK ALONE. We're not . . . fuck you, Morris goodbye. Just . . . stay away from us.

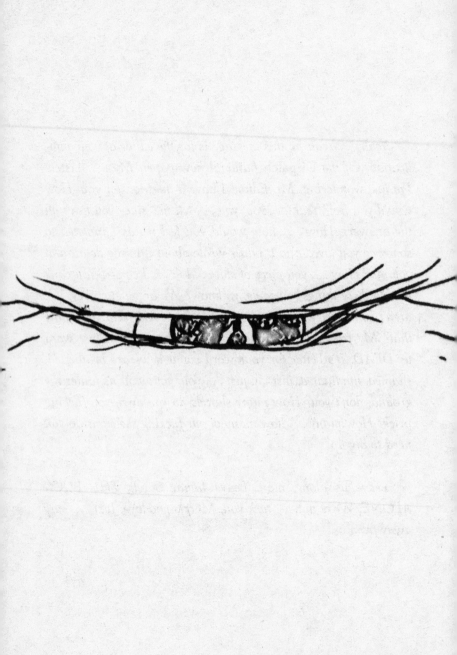

ONE

PEAR KEEPS CALLING. HE KEEPS LEAVING MESSAGES ASKING me to pick up. I can't answer the phone. I'm watching reruns of *Seinfeld*, and the *Dispatch* is in my lap, my face staring up at me.

"Victim."

Who is this person? This victim? Jamar.

Who am I?

   "A source told the *Dispatch* Mr. Sands was found covered in blood and bodily fluids at the scene of the crime, yet authorities stated they found no open wounds

on his body. When reached for comment, Detective Whirloch declined, stating it was an ongoing investigation. The *Dispatch* did, however, confirm from a friend of the victim that the blood and bodily fluids belonged to a deceased cat that was found outside Mr. Sands's apartment."

"The Dispatch *did, however."*
Monsters.
What kind of newspaper talks about itself in the third person?
What friend told them this?
Who would do such a thing?

Below the paper, something moves underneath my shirt. I lift it up and look at all the scars on my stomach, comets caught in ice.

Something sticks out of my belly button. Something thin and pink.

Like a tongue.

It is a tongue.

With not a single suspect arrested in more than a year, Detective Whirloch was released from the case earlier this week. John Oretta, deputy director of the FBI's Violent Crime unit, resumed the investigation, releasing a statement that said in part, "The perpetrator will be brought to justice in a court of law, and I'm here to make that happen."

Mr. Sands was said to have met the perpetrator on the dating app OkCupid, where she went by the username Maude. Earlier this week, the *Dispatch* confirmed an account on the website with the username Maude, registered to one Maude Sands. According to sources, the account has been inactive since January of this year, the month in which Mr. Sands's assault took place. The FBI declined to comment on whether this was, in fact, the account used to lure Mr. Sands and whether it was just a coincidence that the account holder has the same last name as Mr. Sands. In an effort to make contact with the perpetrator, a reporter from the *Dispatch* reached out to the account belonging to Maude for comment. No response has been received.

"Maude Sands?"
She used my name?
Why did she use my last name?
Does she know me?

God. She knows me, doesn't she.

The tongue moves slowly around my stomach, then slips back inside me.

The muscles around my lower back begin to seize.

The whole room reddens raw.

I throw the newspaper on the ground and stare with terror at the sight of it: the black hole where my belly button used to be.

My ribs clench. Teeth mince. More muscles seize. Contract and release.

I am floating in an abyss of absence.

"used to lure Mr. Sands"

I lean forward and look at the hole in me.
Something small and green shines back.

An eye.

It blinks.

I cover my mouth.

The room goes blind, the room no longer seeing me in it.

They reached out to it for comment?
To her?
They went on there and reached out to her?
They tried to talk to her?
Why would they do that?
Why did they fucking do that?

I lean back on the couch. Long, crooked fingers pour out of my hole like spider legs. Its nails are painted red. The fingers spread me. A scalp emerges. Then a head.

It is covered in the meat of me.

It is covered in who I am.

Her wrists steady themselves on my hips and pull her body out from inside mine.

She stands over me, dripping, glazed with the shades of my organs. Her face invisible behind the blood-glass.

I weep and tell her I love her.

I love you.
Is this how you love me?

I do not love her, but she owns me. I have come apart. I am an owning.

She says nothing. She pulls her hair out from the hole in my stomach.

It is longer than an intestine. It is longer than an umbilical cord.

I am exhausted. Broken. Preyed.

She opens her mouth and leans toward mine.

I enter her. She swallows me.

First my face
then my shoulders
then my ass
and my feet.

I slide down into her throat.

My body curls into its self and swings in her warm stomach as she walks.

Where are you taking me, Maude?
What are you going to do with me now?

I am inside her forever.
I am the predator now.
I am the assaulter.

I'm the power now.

Are you going to lock me in your chat room, Maude?
Can I say goodbye to my sister first?

I lie in her body and just listen to her breathe.

When I wake up, the newspaper is still in my lap. The scars still on my stomach.

On TV, someone tells Julia Louis-Dreyfus she looks like she's just seen a ghost.

V

JOSHUA_DISPATCH: Dear Maude, my name is Joshua Greenfield and I am a reporter with the *Dispatch* newspaper. In the event you ever check this OkCupid account again, we would love to get a statement or comment from you regarding your relationship with Jamar Sands, Donald Ellis, or Pear O'Sullivan. Specifically, we would love to hear from you directly regarding your motives. Perhaps one of these men did something to you at one point? Perhaps you have your own history with violent men? Were you yourself ever sexually abused or harmed? Anything you'd like to share with us would be greatly appreciated and would be printed verbatim. Alternatively, if there is anything you'd like to tell us off the record, we are open to that as well. My personal email address, should you not want to leave such a statement here, is Josh.s.greenfield@gmail.com. Looking forward to hearing from you, and thank you for considering this. Best, Joshua

<Maude is offline.>

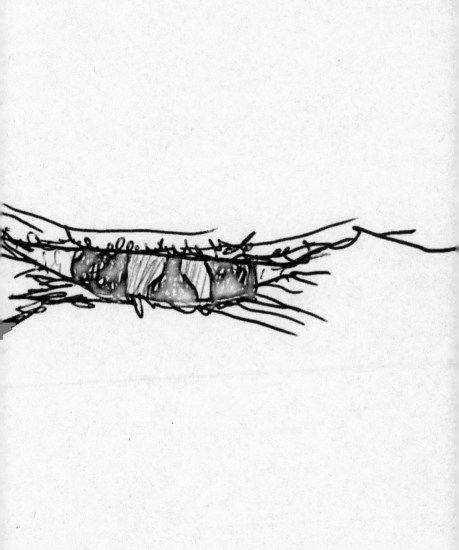

ONE

You know who I am, don't you?

I know you do.

What's your name?

Never mind, you don't need to tell me. I already know.

You know, contrary to what you might think of me, why you might be here, there was a time when I actually loved women. I swear to you. Sebastian White wasn't always an up-tight anti-muff fag, doing Dom Pérignon Jell-O shots on some daddy's yacht off the coast of France. Okay, maybe I haven't done that. *Yet*. But God, a girl can dream. I've always been the loudest queen in the room, who loathes more than he loves. Doesn't everyone? You're such a liar if you say you don't.

Hello? What are you looking for in there, my Pantene? My anal beads?
Just kidding, I don't use Pantene.

God, I can already tell you're no fun.

Just a joke!

. . . Okay. Where was I? Right. Loathing.

There's so much to loathe in this world, wouldn't you agree? Islam. Welfare leeches. Rachel Maddow. Liberals. Sean Penn! Anything with beets in it. Beets are *vile*. But more than any of that, as you know, I loathe feminists. It's by no small miracle that all feminists in America haven't been stoned to death by now. I'm just telling you the truth. Feminists are *pollution*, taking a stance—against what exactly, no one in their right mind knows. They are angry, bitter, saggy chauvinists masquerading as supportive, loving sisters. Feminists—and you women in general—have it easy. *Easy*. Let me tell you. I'm not afraid to say that, even now. You want to see first-world inequality, try growing up a gay man in Alberta, Canada. *Easy*, I tell you. Women by nature need something to complain about in order to feel like they matter. And they are always unhappy. *Always*. To repurpose John Lennon: if you don't believe me, just take a look at the one you're with. They hate their jobs, their fashion, their weight, their husbands, their children, their *lack* of children. Especially this new generation of nonbreeding Chronic Feminists—a term *I* coined—working horrid hours as assistants to prenuptial lawyers or whatever, just to claim some inane independence, while their boyfriends make partner and pay for their rosé, tampons, and pink pussy hats. I wrote an article about it for *The Guardian*. Chronic Feminism is the end of the *real* woman. The end of a well-taken-care-of house, the end of a proper home-cooked meal. The end of marriage. The end of *breast milk*, for God's sake.

I hope you're not a feminist. I can't imagine you are. You're actually *intelligent*.

I don't even have to know you to know that much is true.

I think we can both agree that feminism is for the weak, wouldn't you say?

I can keep talking. Believe me, I can do *all* the talking.

Let me tell you something. You've read my columns, right? Well, when I was younger—before I knew I was a fabulously handsome homo who could live off salad and dick for the rest of my life—I had a girlfriend named Jane. We were sixteen. She was righteously chubby, with a big smile that just sort of fell and broke across her face, like a busted jar of pickled turnips or something. Jane had blond hair the shade of a dove's cunt and used to do her roots with Clorox bleach laundry detergent when she didn't have money. It was insane and fantastic. She had tits so big we used her cleavage as a drug compartment. Her tits were like Halloween; reach in and find some new candy every time. I loved Jane. We met at camp one summer and became inseparable. She taught me how to type, giving me my first writing skill. She taught me many things, honestly—how to sew chiffon, which is a blessed *nightmare*. Jane taught me how to be a straight-up *bitch*. But most important, Jane taught me—no, showed me—the art of the blow job, which would later spin off into various other jobs I fell madly in love with: hand jobs, cushy jobs, bang-up jobs, rim jobs, snow jobs, inside jobs, hum jobs, nose jobs. Looking back, it's obvious Jane was less my honey and more my hag, but I fucked her anyway. As I got older, I became keenly aware of two things: one, I hated having actual sex with her because, two, I was attracted to boys.

You do know I'm gay, right? Not really your type, am I. Just saying.

Anyway, Jane and I dated for two years, until I turned eighteen and the closet was like, "You can't stay in here anymore, dyke, you gotta go." So I broke up with her and came out in an op-ed in *Taki's Magazine*, my *favorite* conservative website at the time. I wrote about being a Gay in Sheep's Clothing, surrounded by a liberal army of unhappy homosexuals who hated me and my beliefs, hated the fact that one of their own was a Libertarian. Perhaps we couldn't agree on immigration reform, I argued, but we could definitely agree on the fact that vaginas are *disgusting*.

I apologize, I know you have one, but honestly, they are.

If you remember, I wrote that it was my sexual life with Jane that first made me keenly aware that I was different. That I didn't enjoy sex with her, but that I likely would never enjoy sex with *any* woman. I didn't use her real name, of course, I'm not a fucking monster. The article got quite the buzz. And why wouldn't it? It was ripe and fresh with *honesty*. And it set me apart from the liberal gay mafia, which is exactly what I wanted. Soon I had offers to write for everyone from *Breitbart News* to the *Humble Libertarian*. It was *thrilling*. I wrote essays, had columns in the *Wall Street Journal* and the *National Review*, became a regular commentator on Fox News—and the rest is, as they say, *her*story.

You do understand, don't you? I'm not a bad person. I'm a *freed* person.

Contrary to that thought, I'm actually fucking decent as hell, *because* I'm honest. Brutally, yes, but come on, don't you find it incredibly refreshing? I mean, wouldn't you rather I tell you I think you're an awful person—You are, by the way, I mean, just *look* at you right now, what you're doing—than lie to you just because I'm scared of how you'll react?

Really ask yourself if anything I've said so far is not true.
It's just you and me here.
It may be cruel. May be hard to hear.
But it's not a lie.

Look, I had to talk about Jane so readers could understand my own personal discovery better. It was an important detail in my trajectory. I always knew I had been attracted to men, but it wasn't until I actually dated a woman that I positively KNEW I was not of the hetero herd.

Why are you here, by the way? Why are you even here? I mean, I know this isn't just random. You clearly *picked* me. *Specifically.* You weren't just walking by. Were you? You weren't. I know you weren't. I'm the perfect fodder for your misandry. Your envy.

You hate me, don't you. You do. You can say it. I know you do. You can say it.

Say it. Say you hate me.

Say: I hate you, Sebastian White.

I loved Jane, you know. I still do. I'll always love her. I know you must've had a Jane in your life at some point, right? Come on. Everyone does. A relationship that expires once someone turns into a Sensitive Lunatic, which, as you know, was the title of my first book. People will completely freak out over your hard-earned success when you least expect it. Jealousy is mercurial. It doesn't always show up the way you think it will. My experience with her also taught me that people's feelings will inevitably get in the way of almost every rational thought or action, if they are allowed to.

Like your feelings right now. Look at you. I can feel it! I can feel you thinking with your *feelings*.

And this is why I protect my intellect and point of view at all costs. This right here. And Jane right there. And every Chronic Feminist I've had to sue for defamation in between. I am a provocateur. I am "priviledged," as the liberal snowflake would like to cry. Yes, I'm priviledged. Priviledged to say whatever the fuck I want to whenever the hell I want to. Free speech, honey. Free. Beautiful. Speech. You must never allow yourself to be censored or silenced by those who get upset easily, by those who are what I call Emotional Polenta—poor

people's food for thought, which was the title of my second book, a *New York Times* bestseller.

All right. I guess you're just going to sit there in silence and judge me, aren't you.

How easy for you to do, considering this position I'm in, separated from you in the way that I am. Considering that you can hear me but I can't hear you. *Because you won't speak.*

You know what that makes you, sweetie? A coward.

Do you think I care?

Hello? Are you still here?

Have I made you angry with what I've said? Do you think I deserve this? I just wanted to explain who I am and give some real context, not fake-news context. If you've read about Sebastian White in the media, then surely you've gotten the wrong impression of who exactly Sebastian White is.

You seem filled with spite, and I don't even know what you look like.
I can feel it, though. Do you spite me?
Is this some sort of vengeance where you'll enjoy my getting what I deserve?

I feel like you're close but you're not answering me on purpose, and now, honestly, honestly now, I'm just getting angry.

Where are you? Are you in the room? Just get this over with, for fuck's sake.

Is that you breathing, or is that the fan?

Hello?

You know what, I don't even care anymore. Do whatever the hell you're going to do to me, darling, I've suffered far worse, believe me. And when you're done, I'll have an incredible story of your pathetic revenge rampage for my next memoir. Which is actually a great title, come to think of it.

I will enjoy *monetizing* you.
I will enjoy seeing you in court when they catch you.
I'll sue your family and friends when this is all over. You know that, right?

You will have nothing. You will—

VI

IV

JAMARVELOUS83: Are you there?

JAMARVELOUS83: I read that a reporter from the *Dispatch* reached out to you for a comment. What are you going to say, Maude? That you're a monster? That you're sick? That it's funny? Are you going to tell them why you did it? Why you did what you did to me? How about you tell me first. Go on. You owe me that much.

Tell me.

Tell me.

Please

Tell me motherfucker why did you do this to me

<Maude is offline.>

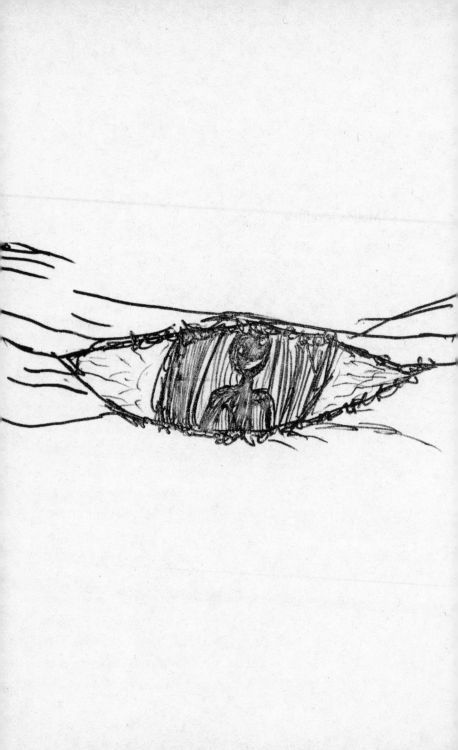

ONE

GOOD EVENING, I'M YOUR HOST, MELISSA HOPE, AND thank you for joining me on BCN's number-one primetime television talk show covering ALL of America's most HORRIFIC stories and injustices, right here on *The Melissa Hope Show*. Our top story tonight: Male. Sexual. Assault. Another BOMBSHELL in the case that's rocked the nation over the last year, as controversial provocateur author and TV personality Sebastian White comes forward as the FOURTH VICTIM to be attacked by an unidentified female predator known to federal investigators only as Maude, whose string of violent crimes against men seems to have NO END in sight. Maude even has her own FAN CLUB, ladies and gentlemen, a vigilante online group who call themselves "The Maudesters." As you know, this pro-

gram landed an exclusive interview with Donald Ellis mere months after his assault and has continued to lead the charge with the most up-to-date information and coverage on this horrifying case as it continues to unfold. Joining me tonight on the Hope Panel: Brenda Landowski, a forensic psychologist and former FBI investigator, now a fellow BCN contributor—welcome to the family, Brenda!—Jennifer Sampson, a criminal defense attorney, and Meryl Pichette, social media critic and blogger at EverythingMen.com. Brenda, let's jump right in: What. The. Hell, Brenda?

BRENDA: Listen, in all my years at the Bureau I don't think I ever saw such a whodunit—no, literally, WHO!—

MELISSA: [*Laughter*]

BRENDA: This . . . this perpetrator has been covering their tracks—

MELISSA:—HER!—

BRENDA: [*Laughter*] Yes! "HER!," thank you—HER tracks incredibly well. I mean, listen, minimal physical and serological evidence, no prints, no witnesses. It's hard not to sympathize with investigators here as they struggle for . . . for anything even remotely resembling a lead. I mean, if I were working these cases, I'd wonder—I'd wonder if I was working with some kind of professional, Melissa.

MELISSA: Chills. I literally have CHILLS here, Brenda. So . . . Give it to me hard, Hope-style: Almost a year now. Four victims: Donald Ellis, Watertown, New York. Pear O'Sullivan, Springfield, Massachusetts. Jamar Sands, Albany, New York. And now Sebastian White, Westchester, New York. That's a stone's throw away from our Manhattan offices! *Utterly terrifying.* No leads. No arrests. No suspects. What's the FBI's next move?

BRENDA: Right, well, as you know, there have been some very disturbing details leaked to the press—

MELISSA:—Yes, tell us about this, Brenda, I mean, they found a SIX-FOOT-LONG HAIR, for Christ's sakes—

BRENDA:—I know!—

MELISSA: I mean, I feel PHYSICALLY. ILL. What kind of hygiene does this Girl Thing have?

BRENDA: [*Laughter*] Yes, well, so many questions remain, Melissa in fact, I would say ALL questions remain. Listen, that hair and whatever else they might have DNA-wise haven't delivered any matches, so I imagine investigators are really scratching their heads at this point. Now, it's possible they may have a suspect they aren't telling us about, but I haven't heard anything from my sources. It's as if this woman just doesn't exist.

MELISSA: What about circumstantial? Tell us about the crime scenes.

BRENDA: I wish there was more to tell, Melissa. I mean, everything I'm hearing sounds, you know, uncompromised. I don't think anyone's handled anything poorly here. There are no signs of crime-scene contamination, there's no—I mean, look, it's frustrating for everyone involved, but this is just one of those cases for the ages, ya know?

MELISSA: You heard it here, folks. One. For. The. Ages. Breaking live. Right here, in your living rooms, ladies and gentlemen. Unleash the lawyer! Jennifer Sampson, come take a dive in Melissa's deep end. Drop your detective anchor: what do you make of these specific cases and the controversial circumstances surrounding how, in particular, they occurred?

JENNIFER: Listen, no one deserves to be the victim of a sexual

assault, but doesn't this bring up another issue, Melissa—

MELISSA:—I knew there'd be a "but"!—

JENNIFER: Yeah, but shouldn't people engage in common-sense behavior? The first victim—

MELISSA:—Yeah. Like don't rape an unconscious person?—

JENNIFER: Melissa, what kind of sense does it make for anybody, a girl or a boy or anybody, to get stinking drunk to the point that—to the point that you don't know what's going on, you have no consciousness about where you are or what you're doing, you're drinking with a random woman at a bar instead of being at home with your *wife* and *kids*—

MELISSA:—Mmm hmm—

JENNIFER:—I mean, shouldn't people engage in some kind of behavior so as not to put themselves in a vulnerable position?

MELISSA: You're absolutely right, but does that negate the fact that while he's unconscious, she rapes him?

JENNIFER: Listen, that's a form of conjecture, Melissa, I don't have to tell you that. I mean, the third victim, Jamar Sands, was in an online CHAT ROOM with this woman! He invited her OVER! They were drinking and engaging in sexual acts consensually, according to the victim's own statement—

MELISSA:—Until it wasn't consensual—

JENNIFER:—We don't know that, Melissa. I mean, it appears the victim was into some strange kinky stuff, with animal masks and this woman and the whole dead-cat thing—

MELISSA: So now you're saying victim number three was a bad boy, he was SUCH A BAD BOY, he needs a spanking! Spank, spank, spank!—

JENNIFER: I'm not saying he was bad, I'm saying it was *poor judgment*—

MELISSA: No, no, Jennifer—let me ask you this, then. What about victim number one, Donald Ellis? If it was consensual, why did this woman just run away and leave Mr. Ellis lying there, half-naked, with blood and dirt all over his privates—

JENNIFER:—I don't know, I don't know, but—

MELISSA:—Why did she do that if it was consensual?—

JENNIFER:—I don't know, but what I do know is that his judgment was seriously impaired, that by his own admission, and scientific evidence, he had twice the legal amount of alcohol in his body—

MELISSA:—There are no mitigating factors when it comes to sexual assault, Jennifer. All right, Meryl Pichette, your chance to tick-tock on the Melissa Hope clock. Now's your time. Jennifer brings up an interesting point regarding being made to penetrate—which is, for viewers at home, the legal term in a court of law for the rape of a man by either a woman or another man. Meryl, tell me what your readers are saying and what you're reading on social media about this SHOCKING story.

MERYL: Well, Melissa, our readers definitely have a lot to say here: the word *Maude* has been trending on Twitter for three days straight, and it's the most-searched term on our website. But, I mean, a lot of people are asking some really tough questions—

MELISSA:—Go on—

MERYL:—Well, it's like, okay, a lot of Americans want to know how, like literally HOW exactly, this could've been rape. I mean, from purely a logical perspective, wouldn't a man have—and I just have to ask this, with all due respect to the victims—wouldn't a man have to get an erection in order to be made to penetrate?

MELISSA: Tough questions, and I applaud you for going in deep here—

MERYL:—Thank you—

MELISSA:—And I'm no expert on the male anatomy and how it functions—

MERYL:—Oh, I am, Melissa, and believe me, I know how it functions!—

MELISSA:—[*Laughter*] You are hilarious, Pichette!—

MERYL:—And there are so many questions, like, for instance, why didn't these men just push the attacker off them? I mean, they're men!

MELISSA: Right.

MERYL: I mean, Mr. Sands is a young, handsome, assumedly strong guy—

MELISSA:—Maybe not so strong after all—

MERYL: Yes, well, yes, obviously, and that's why I'm bringing it up. The American public wants to know why a guy with that kind of physical build, who did kettlebell tournaments, could be subdued by—by a WOMAN. And you know, Melissa, the harder question here—

MELISSA:—Tell me—

MERYL: The harder question here is, why was Mr. Sands aroused in the first place? How is that possible if—

MELISSA:—Right—

MERYL:—If, I mean, if it was *not* consensual? And according to what we've heard so far, she had a nickname for him in the chats they had—she called him Wolf.

MELISSA: That's right, Maude is what she went by in that transcript of the chat obtained by the *Dispatch* earlier this year—

MERYL: Yes, Maude—

MELISSA:—Maude! It's such an awful name. I mean, who IS this creature!

MERYL: [*Laughter*] Yeah, I mean, some people on Snapchat were mentioning that, like, she couldn't have picked, I don't know, like, a better name to go by?

JENNIFER: Reminds me of my great-aunt or something . . .

MELISSA: [*Laughter*] Yes! Maude. More like *Maude* to penetrate!

JENNIFER: [*Laughter*]

MERYL: [*Laughter*]

BRENDA: Maude to penetrate!

JENNIFER: [*Laughter*]

MELISSA:—Seriously! [*Laughter*]

BRENDA: [*Laughter*] Oh, that is too good!

MERYL: [*Laughter*]

JENNIFER: [*Laughter*]

BRENDA: [*Laughter*]

MERYL: [*Laughter*]

MELISSA:—All right, back on the Melissa Hope track, straight and narrow. Meryl, break it down for me: How is Twitter reacting to all this uncertainty? What's the general consensus out there among the top voices in America? Give me their reactions.

TWO

Did anyone watch @MelissaHopeShow tonight?
#MaudeToPenetrate is a stroke of genius. A consensual, nonvio-
lent stroke.
  —Daniel Tosh
  315 comments | 710 retweets | 3.5K likes

.@PulitzerPrize please give @MelissaHope the Big P for naming the lady who did bad things to some dudes.
#MaudeToPenetrate
  —Fat Jew
  35 comments | 170 retweets | 534 likes

My heart breaks for the #MaudeToPenetrate victims and their
families sending so much love and prayers and strength
  —Taylor Swift
  685 comments | 56K retweets | 742K likes

Conflicted about #MaudeToPenetrate Why was this married father of 2 drinking w/ a random woman in the first place?
—Meghan McCain
229 comments | 676 retweets | 2.5K likes

moment of silence 4 victims of #MaudeToPenetrate tonight at my MSG show I am here & will fight 4 u. U are not alone. B strong.
—Lady Gaga
1.1K comments | 38K retweets | 990K likes

Writing a memoir on my horrible experience being attacked by #MaudeToPenetrate stay tuned for updates on publisher, date, etc.
—Sebastian White
110.1K comments | 150K retweets | 280.8K likes

Controversial writer, blogger, and #MaudeToPenetrate victim Sebastian White is writing a book, and we are equally horrified and thrilled.
—*Jezebel*
23.1K comments | 86.2K retweets | 171.2K likes

I'm just going to say it: Men, enjoy a taste of your own medicine. #Maudester
—Laura Marie
115 comments | 610 retweets | 1,233 likes

When it comes to violence against men, some people are actually saying what many have been thinking: Men are getting what they deserve. Inside the bizarre world of #Maudesters

—*Bitch* magazine

64 comments | 301 retweets | 609 likes

Read my latest piece in The Atlantic on a brewing cult calling themselves the Maudesters and how generations of violence and abuse against women has inevitably led to this moment. #MaudetoPenetrate

—Jill Fitzpatrick

115 comments | 610 retweets | 1,233 likes

This Maudesters shit is the scariest witch hunt of them all.

—Feminist Bullshit

77 comments | 324 retweets | 1,001 likes

Young woman drugged and raped on university campus, authorities are looking for a white male in his early 20s. Contact @Chicago_Police with any information.

—*Chicago Tribune*

1 comment | 0 retweets | 1 like

What's worse than #MaudeToPenetrate? #LiterallyNothingIHaveNoJokesThisIsHorrifying

—Jim Gaffigan

699 comments | 23.6K retweets | 232K likes

FALSE: #MaudeToPenetrate is not part animal. At least not that we know of.

—Snopes

1.5K comments | 44K retweets | 200K likes

Can a man be raped? Some say not possible. Join the #MaudeToPenetrateDebate tonight on Facebook Live @ 11:30 p.m. EST

—Facebook

44.6K comments | 100K retweets | 885K likes

Yes, men can get raped. There is no #MaudeToPenetrateDebate, only rape.

—*Teen Vogue*

2.9K comments | 12K retweets | 200K likes

Yo dudes CANNOT GET RAPED. Trust. Not possible. Someone is lying. #HateMaudeToPenetrateDebate

—Kanye West

10.9K comments | 444K retweets | 1.1M likes

I remember when I was told by someone that I was going to get raped for smoking pot

—Leah_Sky_15

0 comments | 0 retweets | 0 likes

My new album is written for the victims of #MaudeToPenetrate. Donate to my Kickstarter album fund today.

—Amanda Palmer

2.9K comments | 8K retweets | 12.8K likes

Simon & Schuster acquires Sebastian White's forthcoming memoir, Revenge Rampage, for historic seven-figure deal.

—*Publishers Weekly*

599 comments | 1K retweets | 4,901 likes

Read Jonathan Safran Foer's new short story, "Maude in the Medusa of a Man's Arousal," in our summer issue.

—*The New Yorker*

139 comments | 123 retweets | 2K likes

How do you politely tell your mother's friend (who is trying to be helpful) "I was raped. It doesn't matter who sleeps in my bed."

-caats4Lyfe

1 comment | 0 retweets | 3 likes

Read my latest piece: The Inequality Game: How we talk about the white #MaudeToPenetrate victims compared to Jamar Sands.

—Shaun King

875 comments | 1.1K retweets | 321K likes

Hold the ones you love near and dear today.
#MaudeToPenetrate
   —Oprah Winfrey
   5.8K comments | 6.7K retweets | 321K likes

Join our #MaudeToPenetrate panel of experts tonight to discuss the heated topic of male rape 8/7 C on @FoxNews
   —Sean Hannity
   4.6K comments | 502 retweets | 111K likes

Pray for the sins of the #MaudeToPenetrate men with us.
   —*National Review*
   401K comments | 467K retweets | 1.2M likes

We will be protesting outside Brown University today, where sinner Donald Ellis will be speaking about sexual assault.
   —Westboro Baptist Church
   15 comments | 33 retweets | 180 likes

Don't worry, we are working with greatest to catch monster Maude! Disgusting! America has best most amazing experts!
   —President of the United States Donald J. Trump
   786K comments | 1.6M retweets | 5.8M likes

BREAKING: Man comes forward as fifth victim in #MaudeToPenetrate attacks.
   —Associated Press
   50K comments | 163K retweets | 1.8M likes

46-year-old Michael Parker of Shelburne, Vermont, is the latest victim in a string of unsolved violent sexual crimes by a female perpetrator.

—BuzzFeed

1.2K comments | 12K retweets | 17.4K likes

Michael Parker says he was violently attacked by #MaudeToPenetrate but many remain skeptical.

—CBS News

8K comments | 81K retweets | 404K likes

Everything you need to know about trans criminal Michael Parker, formerly Michaela Parker.

—*Christian Daily*

36K comments | 222K retweets | 800.1K likes

I'm sorry has anyone seen the arrest sheet on this lady Michaela Parker before she decided not to be a lady anymore? She is a former homeless prostitute. Fake News won't tell you this. #MaudeToPenisRape

—Alex Jones

199 comments | 2.3K retweets | 4K likes

Trannies are mentally ill people who need psychological help, not your sympathy.

#MaudeToPenisRape

—Gavin McInnes

2K comments | 12K retweets | 105K likes

What if Michaela Parker IS Maude and raped herself? Possible since I hear she has a pussy and penis
    —Mike Cernovich
    210 comments | 1K retweets | 215 likes

There is a special place in hell for people questioning Michael Parker's honesty based on his sex assigned at birth. Very special place.
    —Roxane Gay
    444 comments | 555 retweets | 5.6K likes

Maude's all "I'm not going out tonight I'm just gonna stay home, Netflix and rape."
    —Whitney Cummings
    201 comments | 3.9K retweets | 9.9K likes

The news got you down? Exercise will get you up! New Fabletics sportswear for 20% off by using promo code 33447DH now through Sunday!
    —Kate Hudson
    50K comments | 200K retweets | 5.8M likes

Did you know 80% of trans people suffer from mental illness and 3 in 5 have been incarcerated? #FactsMatter #MaudeToPenetrate
    —*Breitbart News*
    2.8K comments | 133K retweets | 453K likes

Investigators still have no leads in #MaudeToPenetrate case, insiders say.

—*Los Angeles Times*

675 comments | 280K retweets | 5.8M likes

Pressure grows to find more evidence on Michael Parker's allegations before counting him as an official #MaudeToPenetrate victim.

—NBC News

7K comments | 16.1K retweets | 31.2K likes

Liberals and conservatives can't even agree on Michael Parker. How can they agree on the national debt?

—*Business Insider*

210K comments | 677K retweets | 2.3M likes

#MaudeToPenetrate victim-turned-activist Donald Ellis holds rally in Watertown to support victims of sexual assault.

—*New York Daily News*

56K comments | 145.1K retweets | 256K likes

Op-ed: Michael Parker: a tricky story with an even trickier narrative. #MaudeToPenetrate

—*Washington Post*

210K comments | 677K retweets | 2.3M likes

You say tomato, I say Michael Parker was not raped. Let's call the whole thing off. #MaudeToPenetrate

—Bill O'Reilly

14.2K comments | 22.5K retweets | 156K likes

I have seen the most awful things tweeted at Michael Parker recently. Do you people have no sense of decency? Leave the man alone.

—Ann Curry

76 comments | 140 retweets | 210 likes

The bullying needs to stop. Michael Parker is a person, not a punching bag.

—Chris Hayes

45 comments | 50 retweets | 176 likes

We must end the gender-shaming of victim Michael Parker. Join the conversation and resist. IRL on Facebook tonight 8/9C #IStandWithMichael #SayHisName

—Women's March

155 comments | 2.3K retweets | 10K likes

On today's show: trans women who have ALSO been assaulted and not believed! Wait till you hear these stories! #IStandWithMichael

—*The Wendy Williams Show*

108 comments | 57 retweets | 1K likes

The best tweets from celebrities about #MaudeToPenetrate victim Michael Parker

—*HuffPost*

26K comments | 117K retweets | 150K likes

Horrified by questioning of Michael Parker's honesty.
I stand with him. Do you? #TransLivesMatter #SayHisName
#IStandWithMichael
    —Katy Perry
    210K comments | 677K retweets | 2.3M likes

Now on sale: "I Stand with Michael" T-shirts, 50% off with your
next purchase!
    —Zazzle
    56 comments | 435 retweets | 553 likes

Katy Perry says she's "horrified" by the treatment of
#MaudeToPenetrate victim Michael Parker.
    —Yahoo! News
    33 comments | 56 retweets | 101 likes

Katy Perry stands up for Michael Parker in touching tweet.
    —*Entertainment Weekly*
    176 comments | 309 retweets | 4.9K likes

Katy Perry pens heartbreaking note to Michael Parker in tweet
supporting trans lives.
    —HelloGiggles
    399 comments | 2.3K retweets | 66K likes

Katy Perry debuts new colorful haircut at concert benefiting
trans victims of sexual assault #MaudeToPenetrate
    —*Daily Mail*
    1.3K comments | 2.8K retweets | 3.9K likes

Katy Perry's hairstylist gives exclusive interview on how the singer's new do sends a political message to the world. #MaudeToPenetrate
—ABC News
340K comments | 1.1M retweets | 2.8M likes

Miley Cyrus dons new hair color inspired by the pansexual pride flag after Katy Perry's recent hair design supporting trans rights.
—CNN
998 comments | 1K retweets | 5.2K likes

5 easy steps to turn your hair into activism by using the LGBTQ+ spray-on stencil! #MaudeToPenetrate
—*Marie Claire*
1.9K comments | 2.4K retweets | 3.3K likes

Michael Parker is the reason we need to protect our innocent children, especially our little girls. Donate now to keep American bathrooms safe.
—Conservative Action Fund
103 comments | 54 retweets | 1.3K likes

Caitlyn Jenner and Jeff Foxworthy come together to discuss both sides of the Michael Parker debate on The Situation Room w/ Wolf Blitzer tonight on CNN.
—CNN
108 comments | 57 retweets | 1K likes

Michael Parker, purported Maude victim and subject of scandal, reported missing by family members.
—*New York Daily News*
12 comments | 52 retweets | 364 likes

If you have any knowledge of the whereabouts of Michaela S. Parker, please call Shelburne Police Department.
—Shelburne Police Department
0 comments | 3 retweets | 20 likes

#MaudeToPenetrate victim Michael Parker found dead of apparent suicide near his home in Shelburne, Vermont.
—Channel 3 News
22 comments | 23 retweets | 129 likes

Amal Clooney shows her flawless curves in a red-hot dress at the G8 Summit.
—NBC News
254 comments | 298 retweets | 355 likes

VII

ONE

"THE WORLD'S GONE BERSERK," I SAY TO JIMMY WHO'S standing behind the bar drying a glass. The news is blaring on a TV, hanging by some bungee cords and old tangled Christmas lights, above him.

"You know that's not safe up there like that, Jim."

"*Nothing's* safe."

I point to my empty glass. *One more.* Jimmy pours me a Scotch. We stare up at the screen. Some newscaster is talking about that freak rapist lady they never found.

"Can't believe it's been five years since all that shit," I say.

"Five already? Crazy."

"Can't imagine being one of those guys, those poor guys she did that stuff to."

"What about that one guy's poor *dick*?"

"Please, Jimmy, don't bring it up. It gives me a tingling sensation—"

"I mean could you imagine having it *rubbed to smithereens*—"

"Jimmy, enough. You're making my balls light-headed."

"I'm just saying, it's my worst fucking nightmare."

"Having no dick?"

"Fuck, man, come on! You're makin' my nuts cramp!"

"At least you *have* nuts, jackoff!"

I throw a pretzel at him. We hear a car coming up the road.

"That better be Lewis with my goddamn drill bits."

"He comin' by?"

Headlights hit the mirror behind Jimmy's head. We look back up at the TV.

"I'll bet stock in jockstraps has skyrocketed."

The bell above the bar door jingles. I look over my shoulder to yell at Lewis. But it's a woman. Alone. Jimmy changes the channel. I lock eyes with him in the mirror. I push my Scotch away and take a sip of water instead.

TWO

O KAY, CLOSE YOUR EYES AND MAKE A WISH."

"Honey, I'm sixty and retiring not six and teething."

"Come on, just make a wish, for your wife."

"You'd like it to be for you, wouldn't you?"

"Thirty years as one of the best cops upstate New York has—"

"Not a *cop*, Alice, a—"

"—*Detective!*"

"—detective."

"Think of everything you've done! Everything you've accomplished."

"Lots I didn't—"

"Make a wish, Mr. Whirloch."

"That's *detective*."

"Detective—"

"—Yeah—"

"Go on, Myles. Close your eyes. Make a wish."

"Can I make more than one?"

"Of course you can, my sweet bear."

"What did you wish for?"

"I wish . . . I wish I could still eat fried food. Wish I didn't have all this cholesterol. Wish I'd punched Robbie Mason in the face back in fourth grade. Wish restaurants didn't put fruit in salads. Disgusting. Wish I didn't lose Papa's army tags in the ocean that year we went to Florida for vacation. Wish I'd buried him with Mom's crucifix, like he'd asked. Wish I hadn't been so selfish. Wish I didn't have bunions so bad, my big toes look like they have smaller toes growing out of them. Wish we'd had one more kid, Alice. Wish I'd made lieutenant. Had more resources at my disposal to . . . to've helped more. To've done more. Wish I could forget some things and remember others.

"Wish that, someday, they find her. Someday soon.

"Wish I had."

THREE

The Decade of Dawning
by Donald Ellis

Dedicated to the life and memory of Michael Parker.

A year goes by. Two. Five.
Every unanswered season spins an ocean of apparitions
inside you.
Ghosts crash like phantom waves, breaking
your mind, a limp swimmer who floats landless.

A new spring sets in,
unsettling your senses,
piercing the mud with needled stems,

shoving life and its living in your face,
making your heart glitter black as a moon's thought.

Another year goes by. Two. Five.
Summer burns spring's hair,
sears its scalp, bloodies its bruising,
blossoms a fresh, boiling despair within you.
You squint your eyes at every female figure,
your pulse lurches, heaving nervous
questions at your skin:
Is that her?

Another year goes by. Two. Five.
Summer cripples into the rippling qualms of fall.
You begin to forget. All the dying leaves of your past
plunge to earth like a star's debris.

There's a cooling. A calming. Your mouth
remembers to brush its teeth,
not the murky memory of its battery.
Pain grows distant but never separate.

Another year goes by. Two. Five.
Winter overthrows autumn and your body
becomes an avalanche of damaged ice
waiting for some crueler, crooked sun.

Every clock's a coffined tock you've grieved.
Your time goes on

but your hands cannot.
If you've learned anything

it's that snow can't be trusted.
One day, your daughter's angels.
The next, a predator's footprints.

You splinter.
Wonder if they'll ever catch her.
See a shadow moving in the river.

Winter, Is that her?

VIII

ONE

GOOD AFTERNOON, I'M DONALD ELLIS AND YOU'RE LIS-
tening to *The Ellis Show*, America's number-one
afternoon radio program here on SiriusXM Radio, thanks to all of you, our listeners and heroes.
Because of listeners like you, we've been able to identify and
catch predators on the run for almost a decade, as well as to
help those who've called in and shared their most difficult
and painful stories to heal. I'm honored to say that over the
past eight years, we've been able to help authorities apprehend
over 460 individuals accused of violent sexual crimes. I've
been merely the conduit for those apprehensions, ladies and
gentlemen, but you—YOU—have done the truly hard work.
You have been the eyes and ears in our country, paying attention and turning in those who wish to harm others. I've said

it from day one of this show, and I'll say it again: American. Citizens. Make. The. Difference. Not me. Not investigators. Not state attorneys. Not prosecutors. Not bureaucrats. Not legislators. You. The people. YOU are the ones with the power. You are the ones who know your communities, know when something doesn't seem right. I believe with all my heart that if someone had been there that night, the night of my attack—a witness—my assault would never have happened. Or if it did, my attacker would've at least been caught. But they never caught her, did they? No, they didn't. They never even *identified* her. She's still out there, a supreme predator, dormant, for now.

And speaking of that awful night . . . I'd like to take a moment to say—to tell you—this is a very big day for me and my family. Very big day. And because of that, this will be a very special program for you listeners. I hope. It was exactly ten years ago today on March second in twenty sixteen that I was violently assaulted and left for—I don't know, dead?—behind a dumpster. Exactly to the day.

For a very long time, I could not speak about that experience. I could not speak at all. I lived in a state of death, a limbo between the past of who I was and the future of what I'd become. I tried to go back to teaching. Tried to go back home, back to my life and my wife and kids. Back to normal. But my world was—it was forever gone. I felt like a sun in a perpetual state of setting. That's the only way I can describe to you how things felt. An unending sense of twilight. Everything I did, everything I said, everything I saw, was dusk. My whole life had turned into impending nightfall. My existence was just caught light, suspended in semidarkness. I quit teaching, at the recommendation of my doctor and my wife. She took care

of me for years after that. Until I could get back on my feet. Until I could, at the very least, learn how to live in that purgatory of shades—not dead, but not *not* dead, either.

And as if the pain of what had been done to me wasn't enough . . . as if the shame and the guilt and the scraps of my broken body weren't constant reminders, my wife and I received hateful letters—death threats, even—from people all across the country, for months. I had "asked for it," they wrote. I was a piece of shit. I was a deadbeat, a sinner, a prick, a pussy, weak, a pansy, a wimp, a candy-ass, a faggot, a bitch, a Mary, a limp dick. They said I made men look bad, or that my wife should divorce me, or that I should probably give my kids up for adoption, or better yet just kill myself so my son wouldn't have to grow up knowing his father was a "cockless coward." That's a direct quote. We had to move to another city. My children had to leave their schools. The bullying . . . It was a cruelty I would not wish on anyone. It was a cruelty I'll never forget.

It ripped me apart, you know. It ripped me apart.

Eventually, I found a sense of living. I found a *way* to live. The more I was able to talk about what had happened—to put into words the actions of that woman—the more I found a small amount of peace. Because of the national attention my case received, I suddenly found myself with an audience and in a position to speak to that audience about the things that mattered most. And what matters are the voiceless.

You know what murder, assault, robbery, false imprisonment, kidnapping, and sexual assault all have in common? They are all considered violent crimes. But only one of those is a deeply intimate crime. Only one places blame on the vic-

tims. Did you know that one in sixteen men in America have been raped? And those are just the ones who have reported it. You know that basketball team you play on after work? You know that birthday party you went to last night? You know that board meeting you had this morning? You know that movie theater you were in last week? Or that cafeteria you're in right now, listening to me talk into your headphones? There is almost a 100 percent chance that at least one person in that room, one person in that meeting or theater, has been sexually assaulted in their lifetime. Approximately 68 percent of all sexual assaults go unreported, according to RAINN. Sexual assault is the single *least*-reported violent crime. And when it *is* reported, the victims are blamed and shamed. Or not believed. Or silenced. Punished. Or their attackers are never prosecuted at all.

Do you know how many backlogged rape kits are just sitting on police-station shelves in America, waiting to be tested? Rape kits *filled* with evidence? Ten thousand kits in Cleveland. Four thousand in Ohio. Four thousand in Illinois. Eleven thousand in Detroit alone. *Twenty thousand* in the state of Texas. Over seventy thousand in total, that we know of. Only six states have laws requiring agencies to send in these kits to crime labs to be tested. *Six. States.* So why should victims come forward, when they see statistics like this? When they see they aren't a priority? When they see that finding and prosecuting a sexual predator is not on any law-enforcement officer's to-do list?

This is why I speak, ladies and gentlemen. Why I fight. Why the work we do here matters.

We have something very special for you today. It fills me with a lot of hope and joy and, of course, anxiety. We have a very special guest with us on the program today: Jamar Sands. His name might sound familiar to you. Jamar, if you recall, was also a victim of Maude almost a decade ago. He and I have become acquaintances over the years, but this will be our first time speaking together publicly. It's important for both of us to keep this story alive. As long as that woman is out there, we will not give up.

So stick around, we'll be right back after this break.

TWO

NO ONE WANTS TO HEAR ABOUT THE BEGINNING. THEY want to hear about the middle or the end. And while I can't tell you what the end looks like just yet, I can tell you about the middle.

My sister, Jen, was pounding on the window, screaming my name. Jamar, open the fucking door, she said. I couldn't open the door because I couldn't stand up. One of the many bummers of living in a smaller town is that everyone knows everyone, so of course the chick I bought razors from at the grocery store was Courtney, who had been roommates with Jen at the College of Saint Rose. Open the fucking door now or I'll break the Goddamn glass, she yelled.

Let me back up for a second. To the beginning of the middle. I feel like I can't justify the end of the middle, and certainly not the beginning of the end, unless I tell you about the beginning of the middle first.

It had been exactly two weeks since the police had come and gone. The FBI dude had come and gone. My family had come, and I'd wished they'd gone. I was sitting alone in my kitchen with a peeled orange on my plate. Eat, dude. Eat. But this orange, this orange looked different than other oranges. Than other foods entirely. All the white strands hung off it, like the pubic hairs of an albino or something. An albino woman. *Woman.* The word tasted abandoned. And the texture of that orange, when I touched it, was so . . . human and rough. It's what I imagined we feel like, right beneath our skin. Rough. Not soft at all. Everything right beneath the skin has such a soft name, you know? Gland. Fat. Nerve. *Soft* tissues. But I'll bet the underneath isn't all that soft. Like, not just bones but also cartilage and muscle and tendon. We're not soft inside. I think people confuse the interior body's sliminess for softness.

My palms were sweating. I couldn't really feel my feet. That fucking orange, man. Just sitting there, in front of me, exposed, skinless. I could *feel* its exposedness, its pulpy insides. It would be so easy to touch it. I could stick my thumbs in through its stomach and rip it wide open if I wanted to. So I did. The sound of it coming apart, of its pieces separating, like a sheet of paper ripping or a heavy exhalation, was enough to make me sick. All its scattered pieces of peel, ripped from its body on the plate. I remember all my scattered clothes ripped

from my body on the floor. She moved on me, that bitch. The memory was so strong. I just passed out right there. I just passed out right there onto the floor.

For weeks, I couldn't eat anything with a peel. I told no one about this. People eating bananas in public made me nauseous. Pretty soon, anything at all that needed to be peeled was just sickening. Tamales, shrimp, garbanzo beans, some types of lettuce. The minute I thought about having to remove some kind of layer, some kind of skin off a food, I was done. I was in a public restroom gagging, or in my car trying to calm the hell down.

I needed to fix this problem I was having with food, I told myself. It dawned on me that I could just stop eating those things. I completely had the right to do that, without questioning myself or losing my shit every time my mom offered me some sad-ass scalped avocado. I could just say no. "The mind is the master and the body is the servant." That's kettlebells 101. So I made the conscious decision to discipline my eating in the way I discipline my training. Mind over matter. Once I gave myself that permission, the nausea, the anxiety—the anger over feeling out of control—just went away. Everything was so much clearer. My protein shakes didn't really need to have banana in them, or any fruit, for that matter. Pretty much every fruit has a peel on it of some kind. And almond milk had to go, because almonds also have a kind of skin. And of course, by this same logic, things like spinach had to go. Spinach is from a flowering plant, and that's just—that's a lot of different kinds of skins, when you think about it. Petals. Leaves. All of that had to go. Plus, I'd read somewhere that scientists had recently figured out how to transform spinach into

human heart tissue, tissue capable of *beating*. I wasn't going to eat that. No fucking way was I going to eat that. I started investigating other plants as well, other types of greens. Kale, for example. Once I started doing my research, I couldn't believe what I found. Kale is actually part of the cabbage family, and cabbage sprouts these beautiful yellow and white flowers, and cabbage leaves protect their inflorescence like—you guessed it—like a kind of skin. So kale was out. Cabbage was definitely out. Parsley, romaine, red leaf, mustard greens, arugula, endive, chard. All of it. Anything leafed. How could anyone in their right mind eat something that once had leaves, I thought. Leaves are part of a vascular system that nourishes a plant or flower, either by sheltering its insides or by absorbing sunlight and oxygen and stuff. *Skin.* Everywhere I looked, I saw skin.

What edible substance *didn't* have a skin, I wondered. It goes without saying that all meats and fish were completely out. Nuts were out. Corn had husks. Peas had pods. Cheese had rinds. Oysters had shells. Skimmed milk sounds like *skinned*.

The next few months were filled with a fresh happiness and sense of purpose, the kind I'd never felt before. By cleaning out my body, I was cleaning out the trauma I'd experienced. All thoughts of what happened to me had been replaced with a newfound understanding of the world and my place in it. I couldn't believe the shit I'd been putting into my body. The cruelty. Everyone was so happy with how quickly I had bounced back, even though they didn't really know why or how. They never asked. But if they had, I would've said: "Success is the sum of small efforts, repeated day in and day out."

I returned to kettlebell training and maintained my healthy way of eating. I made some exceptions for things like condiments. Mustard was actually a fantastic food for me to eat. Yes, a mustard plant has leaves and flowers, but the seed itself doesn't need to be peeled, you see? So that was totally fine. Now ketchup, on the other hand—ketchup comes from tomatoes, and tomatoes most definitely have a skin on them. So I allowed myself some small exceptions. For lunch I could have as many tablespoons of mustard as I wanted, but I could only have one teaspoon of ketchup per day. And cottage cheese was all right to eat, believe it or not, though I kept my portions very small just in case. Just in case some newfound information about rennet or curds was discovered. Cactus was a good one, too. Cactus have flowers, but no *leaves*. So you see, I made some exceptions here and there. I wasn't totally rigid. And bread was safe, although I didn't want to eat too much of it. A typical lunch would look like this: half a cup of cottage cheese, half a slice of bread, three tablespoons of mustard, and one teaspoon of ketchup, which I put directly into my mouth only after the SaS foods had been swallowed, so as not to contaminate them with the ketchup. SaS foods are what I called Skinless and Safe foods. Just a quick way for me to identify them.

I began to see a major change in my body. In a good way, I thought. I was losing all my body fat and becoming toned. I used to be ripped, but I didn't want to be ripped anymore. I wanted to be toned. I wanted to be lean and strong.

My sister grew extremely suspicious. She would leave work early and come surprise me at my apartment with my favorite takeout. What used to be my favorite takeout. But my sister

knows I've always hated surprises. I would tell her I already ate. I'm worried about you, she'd say. She handed me a pamphlet she'd picked up. Some therapy group for guys in town. Specializing in trauma and PTSD. I thanked her and said I would check it out. I was never going to do that. No fucking way, man. And looking back, knowing my sis, she knew I wasn't going to, either. So she kept an eye on me. Checked in daily.

Jen was my older sister by almost six years, and she had always been super-independent. She was the cool punk-rock girl in school who all my friends drooled over. She had thick black curly hair and green eyes. Green eyes came from my mom's side of the family, the hair from my dad's. Because we're mixed— Haitian on my father's and Irish on my mother's—Jen had this look about her that some dicks would call "exotic." I fucking *hated* that, growing up. When guys called her that. Call my sister "exotic" again, motherfucker, I'll break your mouth. Jen could hold her own, though, she didn't need me to be some thick-headed little bro jock for her. I tried, but it was always the other way around. Jen was always the one looking out for me. Always.

I gave in to Jen's surprise takeout dinners after I ran out of excuses and was afraid she'd tell Mom or something. But not without self-imposed consequences. After she'd leave, I'd get an overwhelming sense of dread. A sick feeling in my entire body. It was like I had poisoned it by eating all that trash. I knew I had to get it out of me, but I hated throwing up. I really hated that. So I went into the bathroom and got a razor out. I was sweating and couldn't see very well. I made a small cut in my stomach. Just a small one. The second I saw blood come out, I became calm. I could feel the poison coming out of me. I could almost feel it leaving me. I cried. It was the first time

I'd felt relief in a long time. This became the perfect solution to my dinners with my sister. It also allowed me to start eating with friends again. To start going out again. I could eat SaS as I normally did, but if I was forced to eat a non-SaS food, like if someone ordered something for the table or whatever and I didn't want things to be awkward, I could have a couple of bites of that non-SaS food and just release the poison from my stomach later. These weren't deep cuts I was making in my stomach. They were just small ones. Enough to let the contamination out but not to, like, send me to the hospital or anything. My favorite Dwayne Johnson quote about training is, "It's you versus you." Meaning, you're the only thing standing in your own way. You're the only thing you're up against. So I got even stricter with my SaS diet when I wasn't out with friends or family—when I didn't have to put on a show for them. I cut out cottage cheese and a few other SaS items I used to be allowed to eat. I drank tons of water. More than I'd ever drank before. Water was very safe.

I felt that if I didn't keep the poison out of me, she could appear. If I stopped caring about my health and what I put into my body, she could appear. If I ate too much, she could appear. If I stopped working out, she could appear. If I had less than the required amount of water per day, she could appear. She could appear. She could appear. She would appear.

Then one day, she appeared.

I hadn't eaten in two days. Only water and mustard. I was doing great, I thought. Me versus me, and I was winning. In

the mornings I would get up and do one hundred crunches, no matter how much a fresh, open cut on my stomach hurt. In the mirror, the little scars swam across my ribs, and my ribs swam across whatever was left underneath, and I felt safe. I was disappearing here in this world, which in some way meant I was reappearing somewhere else. I was whole somewhere else. I was free somewhere else. That thought was comforting. The parallel me had never been raped. Had never been touched. Had never been so obscenely violated. The parallel me had no restrictions. Still enjoyed sunlight. The parallel me had a future that couldn't be darkened by his past.

I went to my computer to do some work. I opened my old OkCupid account, and looked at the list of screen names and saw hers there, offline. This is something I did once in a while—checked in to see if she was, you know, around. I never told anyone, though. I'd go online and just . . . *stare*. Stare at that screen name. Maude. *Maude.* It was always offline, but there she was, regardless. There she was, so close, as if on the other side of a door, waiting for me.

She never knocked that night we met. She had told me in our chat that she would be there at midnight on the dot, and to just open the door at exactly 12 a.m. Leave all your lights off, she said. Let's play.

The apartment-building light was bright behind her when I opened the door.

There was a silhouette of a mask. A wolf mask.

She was carrying a plastic bag. I thought I could see her nails. They were either nails or bones.

She came in faster than a wind and shut the door
behind her.

We were in the darkness from the moment she entered.

She put her finger against my mouth. No talking.

We didn't speak. I had been told not to speak.

We ate in silence.

She opened a bottle of liquor in silence.

She placed my hand on the stereo in silence.

We danced to classic rock in silence.

She took me to the bathroom.

She drew a bath.

She washed me.

She put my hand on her thigh.

She bit me.

In the dark.

The silence.

Her mouth was the softest I'd ever felt. But her face, her
face felt like some kind of coarse crust. Like bridge iron. Like it
had a thick coat on it. A second skin.

Skin.

Can we turn on the lights? I want to see you.

You don't want to see me, Wolf, you want to feel me.
You want to feel me, don't you.

Her voice wasn't even in the room.

Her voice was coming from inside me.

Her hands held my wrists down. She started to hum. The world vibrated. Her hands were strong and cold and they held me against the couch with ease.

Just let me, Wolf. Let me do it.

No, hang on, I want the lights on. Please don't.

But she kept going.
And I let her.
I let her.

My sister, Jen, was pounding on the window, screaming my name. Jamar, open the fucking door, she said. I couldn't open the fucking door because I couldn't stand up. I had opened my stomach with a razor blade from as far around my back to the front of my body as I could possibly reach and cut. I had peeled myself open. Like an orange. Not deep, but deep enough to get the poison out. To get her *voice* out.

Just hours before, I had read that she raped another man. His name was Sebastian.

There were no details, but I didn't need the details. I knew whatever she had done, she had done it dreadfully. I imagined the worst. She stuck objects inside him and made him guess. She poured animal urine in his mouth and made him guess.

She wouldn't let him look at her. She laughed and called him a crybaby. She grunted as she came, like some dying pig. She left, as if she'd only come by to borrow some salt. As if she hadn't just taken his life away and left him barely lived.

I was ready to die as my sister's fist came smashing through the glass.

THREE

CALLER, YOU'RE ON THE AIR, THIS IS DONALD ELLIS."

"Hi Donald, name's Nathan, calling from Oklahoma. Nathan without a last name, if that's okay."

"Hey Nathan thanks for calling in. What's your question?"

"It's not a question, really. I just want to thank you and that fellow, Jamar, you just had on the program. It gave me hope. Hearing him talk about his recovery, about how his sister found him there like that, ya know? Almost dead like that on his couch, split open? I mean, praise be. But the part after, where she got him to the hospital in time and saved his life, and how she got him to go to that therapy place where he befriended that other guy—the guy named after a fruit?—it's a good thing. It's a good thing to have a happy ending like

that. It's a beautiful thing. Brought tears to my eyes. And it is a choice, you know? Living. Like that young man said. Just like dying can be a choice. And I really could relate to that thing he said about living with the anger and all that. That it's okay to not accept what happened, to find no resolve but still live a parallel happy life. A life adjacent to the things you cannot forgive. I really liked that. That spoke to me."

"Indeed, Nathan, it is a choice. Indeed. Thank you for calling us today.

"Go ahead next caller, you're live on *The Ellis Show*."

"Nancy calling from San Francisco, California."

"Hi Nancy! How's the fog treating you today?"

"Colder than a witch's tit, as they say, Don! Colder than a witch's tit."

"Ha!"

"Anyway, listen . . . Wow, Donald, I can't believe I'm actually on the air with you right now! I'm a big fan and have been listening to your show for five years now, and though I've never called, I just had to call today to tell you how wonderful this interview was. Wow. How powerful. I was driving across the Golden Gate Bridge in horrible traffic when Mr. Sands talked about his wedding and Mr. O'Sullivan being his best man. I mean . . . I was sitting there in traffic and I was . . . and the sun was going down like it always does here beyond the bridge, and I just burst into tears, you know? It got me thinking, Mr. Ellis. It got me thinking really hard."

"Tell me, Nancy. About what?"

"Well I have three boys who are all grown up now—all very successful, might I add! Proud mama over here!—but

hearing Mr. Sands just made me really think about how I contribute. In both the negative and positive sense of the word. I realize, more than ever, we need to keep fighting and protecting our kids, not just from predators but also from a society and a culture that feels kind of predatory ya know? I mean, that lady did the crimes, but we publicized it. We capitalized on it. We exploited it for ratings or whatever, for stories, with our memes and GIFs and tweeting and all that. We jump on the train. We show their pictures on live TV. We make clever hashtags. We find ways to, like, absolve ourselves from responsibility or say we've helped out with a retweet or something. We've helped because we've mentioned an injustice in passing to our neighbor and we both got to shake our heads. We've helped because we painted a sign. Like, I look at my boys and I think, what if this had happened to them? Or worse . . . what if any of them had done this to someone? And it made me realize that my job as a mother is never done. I must always—ALWAYS—teach them how to treat women. Even as grown men. That is how I can contribute. That is how I can really help."

"This is such a great point Nancy and I believe it's on all of us to think this way—to be introspective this way and ask ourselves the hardest questions we've ever had to ask. Thanks for calling in."

"Caller, you're on the air, this is Donald."

"Hey Donald, my name is Eric, from Arizona. Born and raised."

"Hey Eric from Arizona! What's your question for us today?"

"Well, first, thank you so much for having Mr. Sands on

your program today. I was laughing and also crying when he told the story about Mr. O'Sullivan giving that poor toast at his wedding and bombing with his bad cake jokes."

"Yeah that got me good too, Eric."

"Yeah, I bet, buddy. The crying part came, for me, when Mr. Sands talked about his son. Naming his son Pear last year after Mr. O'Sullivan passed away from cancer. I wanted to say, as a survivor of suicide myself, as a person who made it through two attempts, who still sometimes wonders, who sometimes just wonders if it would've been better, you know? To've followed through? I wanted to say that Mr. Sands's perspective on life, and cheer despite—despite all of that, made me feel less alone. I do hope Mr. Sands goes through with that tree-planting ceremony to honor his friend. I liked that a lot."

"Me too, Eric. I never met Pear but talked to him once over the phone many years ago. I tried to get him to come out and protest with us but I got the sense he wasn't ready for that. Even on that short phone call, I could tell he was very funny and very kind. Whether he believes it or not, he'll be missed by many. So many."

"Hi there, caller, this is Donald."

"My man, Donald!"

"Hey! My man . . . who's my man here?"

"Ronnie, man! From Pittsburgh!"

"Oh Jesus, Ronnie! Why didn't I recognize your voice?"

"Got a little cold, man. Makes me sound like a real baritone."

"I'll say. Thought I was talking to Barry White's grandfather for a second."

"Ha well I could be, let me tell you, I'm older than cloth wiring brother, let me tell you."

"That is old, Ronnie. Very old."

"Listen, D . . . What a show, man, what a show. I hope you have that brother on again, man. I'm sure you're getting a million calls right now, man, but let me just say quickly that I've worked at a crisis center for almost a decade now, man, and I can't tell you how important this kind of work is, man. Even if you never share it publicly like my man Jamar just did, even if you never make a thing out of it publicly, it's so important to do the work and take care of yourself. I hope folks come out of the woodwork today because of Jamar's story. I hope they come out, if they've been sexually assaulted or experienced anything that made them feel like they need to hide. Or they can't speak. They can go to RAINN.org and get lots of information on the steps they can take for self-care."

"Yeah self-care is the motto! I say it and practice it all day, every day."

"Yeah, man. The bottom line, like I always tell my patients, man, there are many things in this world that are not on your side, especially after being raped. The law is not on your side. Public perception is not on your side. Sometimes your own body isn't even on your side. But I'm on your side, man. I'm on your side, and clinics are on your side to help you do you. To heal what you can and say fuck all to the rest. Shit, sorry, can I say fuck on the air? Shit, I just said shit, too. Man!"

"Damnit Ronnie, last time I told you I wasn't going to cry the next time you called but now I can feel the tears coming on . . ."

"I always get you, man, I got your number, man!"

"That you do, friend. You've been listening—"

"—to you for almost eight years, damn straight I have, D, and I'm looking forward to you and that book you promised us you'd write one day. You and your novel, man. I hope you get back into that glorious writing of yours again, it's what you were born to do, brother."

"Thanks Ronnie. That means a lot."

"Alright next caller, you're on the air."

Hi. Hey. My, um, my name's Ezra. Ezra Fisher. I'm calling because . . . I'm calling from Somerset. Somerset State Correctional. I'm an inmate here, so thank you for taking this call. I've been here for two years on charges . . . On robbery and aggravated assault and . . . and some other things. I'm calling . . . I'm calling because . . . thank you, Mr. Ellis. For your show. For your . . . for everything you do. I listen to your show here when I get the chance. A few months ago I read the op-ed you wrote in the Prospect Times, the one where you gave us, like, a good spell to cast on ourselves? I felt like . . . I felt like you were speaking directly to me, Mr. Ellis. I did. And, like, I know we never met before, but . . . I guess today I wanted to tell you something. I'm ready to tell you something. That . . . that I was assaulted. By her. But I never told no one. I never told. And I probably should've, you know? I should've, because I saw her, Mr. Ellis. I saw her face.

To whom it may concern:

I looked up Last Will and Testament online last night to find examples of how to write one. I found a few various forms and also a porn movie about a guy named Will and a guy named Testament and . . . you get the idea. Anyway, my name is Pear O'Sullivan and I'm dying of cancer. But you already know that, because you're the person who will allocate my nonsense after I'm gone! I don't have much, but what I do have matters to me, so what the hell. Maybe it will matter to someone else as well. Okay, here we go.

To my ex-wife Patricia Lorenzo I give my collection of 45s, LPs, CDs, and vinyl. She hated me but she loved my record collection. X's Los Angeles, rare R.E.M., the Quadrophenia soundtrack. She especially loved my comedy vinyl, for some reason. Richard Pryor, Dick Gregory, Lenny Bruce, Joan Rivers, David Cross, Hicks, of course. Give them all to her. She deserves them.

To Bobby M. Johnson from group, I give my forest-green '95 Toyota Camry. It is the ugliest piece of shit ever created and still the most reliable. Just like you, Bobby.

To my mother, Pearl Olympia O'Sullivan, I am sorry you outlived your only son. This should happen to no mother, ever. I am sorry I never made much of myself or gave you grandkids

or could buy you a house. Please know that despite everything that happened in my life, I loved you so much and I was happy. At the end of it all, I went happy. Jesus, this is starting to sound like a suicide note, okay, so to Pearl I give my collector's items, which include my collection of bobbleheads, comics, and my American silver quarter from 1970. Ma, DON'T SPEND THE QUARTER, okay? Please tell this to my mother! The quarter is extremely valuable due to a misprint, and you can get good money for it. Those idiots in the Treasury were so cheap they decided to use Canadian quarters from 1941 and print over them, so if you look closely at the back side of the '70 quarter where the American eagle is, you'll see a "41" ever so slightly coming through.

Sell all these things, Ma. (Except the quarter.) Then I can say I bought you a home.

To the Upper Valley Haven social services organization in Vermont, I give all my furniture, clothing, and kitchen items, except for one thing, which is listed below.

To Pamela from group, who made the best waffles I ever had. Thank you for your kindness over the years and for making a bunch of rejects feel like kings. To Pamela, I give all my potted plants and flowers. Including my teal sweetbay magnolias. Side note, Pam: If for some reason I'm not found for a few days—my body—and those magnolias have died, please do NOT throw them away. It is my wish to be cremated with them.

Speaking of which, it is my wish to be cremated. Please place my remains in a Coca-Cola cup and leave me under a bleacher at Fenway Park during the next World Series. I mean it. Don't take me out after the game. Leave me there and just

let me be swept away with the empty beer bottles and hot-dog wrappers. That trash always made me so happy. Made me feel like I was in a place where people were really living.

To my neighbor Alison Beckett, I give my house, the only property I ever owned. It is small and worth nothing, I know, but it's my intent that it be turned into a library/museum for artifacts, photographs, letters, and any memories from our community pertaining to Maggie the Magnificent Maple Tree. This is the greatest apology I have to offer, Mrs. Beckett. You might be wondering why I am apologizing, but let's just leave it at this offering.

To Jamar Sands, my friend, who is expecting his first kid, a kid I hope I get to meet before I leave this clogged artery of an Earth, I give all my journals. All of them. It is my hope that you find some funny bedtime reading in there for your little guy or girl, whatever she or he will be named. I miss you already, man, and I'm not even dead yet!

I miss you. Love you, Bud.

Last and definitely least, to the woman known as Maude, if they ever find her, please send my broom's handle to her in prison with a note saying, "I'm waiting for you here in hell, Maude. I've saved you a cot right next to me, for eternity."

Sincereless,
Pear Ronald O'Sullivan

ONE

WASN'T PLANNING ON ENDING UP IN HERE AT TWENTY-TWO YEARS old. None of us ever are. I always gotta say that out loud to people because I feel like they see me, my record, they see these tattoos, and they think, "Yeah, he was a bad kid." I was never a bad kid. Ever. I was into cars. Model cars. I had a collection of everything from Volkswagens to Ferraris. I grew up in Warren, Pennsylvania, lived in a nice neighborhood. Middle-class. White parents with some money, not a lot but enough. Happy kid. Outgoing kid, and all that. I was going to grow up and sell cars. Vintage ones. I was going to take shop. I was going to know a car inside and out. That's the kind of kid I was. I had plans. Lots of friends, you know. My best friend's name was Arthur Milwaukee, like the city. Man, I haven't seen Arthur in a long time. Arthur was a redheaded retard. I don't mean a

retarded retard, he was just a retard. You know what I mean. A dumbo who got in trouble for bringing whoopee cushions to class like we lived in the 1950s or some shit. Arthur and I walked home from school together every day. He called me Rezzy instead of Ezra. So that was my nickname. Rezzy. We loved playing *Final Fantasy* and basketball. We didn't know a damn thing about basketball, though, or how to play it. We'd get big glasses of milk from the fridge and take our shirts off and take turns running around in circles like dying chickens, then throw the ball into the hoop. We didn't mind not knowing the rules. We made up our own most of the time. Arthur and I always had Saturday sleepovers. Me at his or him at mine. Arthur and Ezra. That was us. The car kid and the retard.

One New Year's Eve, Arthur's parents were having a party. They had some weird friends over, you know, wearing lots of turquoise and shit. East Coast hippies. Wasn't a big party, but enough for us to stay up and go unnoticed past midnight. I went to the bathroom to go pee, but the door was locked so I used the one in Arthur's parents' bedroom instead. That one was always strictly off-limits, but I really had to go. I was in the middle of peeing when I heard the door open and close. Before I could even turn around, there was someone there. Behind me. They put their hands on me. On . . . She took me, by my . . . she held it and took my hands off it, as I was going. She held it like that, from behind me. She asked me what my name was but I couldn't speak. She asked again. I told her Ezra. She said it was nice to meet me, that I could call her anything I wanted to. I didn't want to call her anything. I wanted her to let go of me. She asked me if I liked girls. I said I guess.

She asked me if I like to play games with girls. I said I didn't know. She asked if she could play with me. She asked if I liked it, her holding me like that. She asked if I wanted her to pull on it gently.

I've never said this to someone out loud.

I'll just . . . tell you that she made me have sex with her, okay. She told me I had to or she was going to hurt my mom and dad. She told me I could never tell anyone because she'd come back and hurt me and hurt my family. She made me promise.

She told me I could turn around and look at her, but then I had to go climb on the bed and not say a word. I had to be quiet or else I'd get in trouble. She said if my friend's parents found out what I was doing in their bedroom they'd be really angry with me.

Turn around, she said. I was crying and shaking. Don't cry, she said. I'm not going to hurt you. I just want us to have fun. I'll be very gentle. I didn't want to, I said. Come on, she said. Turn around and look at me. I turned around.

She was just a normal woman.
She had brown hair and brown eyes.
She wasn't pretty. She wasn't ugly.
She wasn't really old but she wasn't young either.
She was just a normal woman.

Do you know who I am, she asked me.

I told her no.

Good, she said.

After she did what she did, she told me to count very slowly to whatever age I was and not move until I was done counting, and she left. I did the count twice because I was so scared it wasn't enough time. It would've been only a count to ten.

I was only ten years old.

She hadn't lied when she said she wasn't going to hurt me. She didn't. She was gentle. I said nothing. I think I held my breath the entire time. I just stared up at the ceiling. There was nowhere else to look. I remember feeling like . . . like if I didn't move, if I just stared at the same spot on the ceiling, that I wasn't even there, in the room. That I had disappeared. I could see where Arthur's parents had water-damage stains above us. Big brown circles mapped across the ceiling. I traced the lines. Imagined they were different things each time. A race-car track. A dying snail.

I left the room and went downstairs. She was nowhere. Everyone was drunk and laughing. Arthur was asleep on the sofa. I was fucking mad. He should've come looking for me. Why didn't he come for me?

That night I had a nightmare. I have it often. I've had it so many times, I know it by heart now. I can see it backward and forward. It's part of my reality, even here in jail, that dream is more real than prison.

In the dream, we are back in that bathroom. I turn toward

her. Her face has every face in it. It's everyone I've ever known or seen or imagined, combined into one monstered offering. Her hair is everywhere. All over the room, running down into the drains of the sink and bathtub and even overflowing out the window in the other room. It covers houses next door. And mountains in the distance. It's alive. Her hair. And she is so tall. Her shoulders touch the roof. Her head is small and unnatural and bobs across the ceiling, looking down at me. Her eyes move rapidly on her face like caught flies trapped under glass. Her chin is bigger than the width of her body and has no skin on it. Like some kind of whale's mouth. She has no lips but a kind of hole in the middle where . . . where plantlike vines grow from her mouth and hang down. But they aren't real plants, they are some kind of flesh. Strings of flesh. Flesh vines; thick, mossy nerve endings. And at the ends of those vines are flowers. Beautiful flowers covered in drool, drool dripped from her mouth. When she talks, the vines jiggle like she's an earthquake rattling a potted plant or something. She tells me to get in bed. I walk through a giant unseen spiderweb that spreads across my face. *The spider's already inside me*, I think. *It's already inside.* Then I wake up.

I went back home and said nothing to my parents the next day. I couldn't go to the bathroom by myself anymore, but I said nothing about why. Couldn't be alone, ever, for any reason. I didn't sleep over at Arthur's anymore. The more hurt he'd get, the angrier I'd get. I felt it was kinda his fault. I stopped hanging out with him altogether. Once he asked me why I was so mad all the time, so I punched him. It felt good to do that, to punch something. The school counselor asked

me why I did it. My parents asked me why I did it. Arthur asked me why I did it. But I never told them. I made a promise to her that I would never tell.

I traded out Rezzy for a new nickname, EZ, short for Ezra. I made new friends. My best one was a fat, short kid named Marley who we called Fat Short Kid. Fat Short Kid had a dad who smoked, so he'd steal cigarettes for us. First cigarettes a little, then on to the better stuff, stuff his older cousin could get for us. It helped me feel blank. Helped me forget stuff for a little while. By twelve I was already a different person. I mean, I was a different person the minute I walked out of that bedroom that night, but by twelve I was even more different. I cut school all the time. I got into a couple more fights, got suspended. My mother was a mess. By the time I was fourteen, I was the local fuckup. I was *that* kid, the kid all the neighbors feared. I was the bad seed, waiting to sprout. My pops barely talked to me and I thought, good, fuck you anyway. You weren't there for me. You did nothing. Fat Short Kid and me started selling instead of just smoking. At first it was weed, then we moved on. Moved up and all that. Fat Short Kid's parents had enough and sent him to boarding school. I remember his dumpy face with that mole near his lip, waving goodbye to me from his mom's truck as they left school forever. I never saw Fatty again. I felt like anyone I cared about was taken away from me or didn't care to stay. Jim Beam was the only friend I had left. Whatever was in whoever's liquor cabinet.

I was getting drunk in my bedroom alone one night—I think I was sixteen by then. My mom would do searches of my room, looking for shit, but she never thought to check my old model car collection. The hoods could pop open on some of

those joints, so I stashed my shit in there. And any liquor I'd put in a flask inside my homework binder. Anyway, I was getting drunk this one night, alone, and decided to sneak out. I ran down the street looking into the windows of other houses. I thought about going into one. Fuck it, I thought, I'll just try the doorknob and see. Of course it was unlocked. Everyone kept doors unlocked in my old hood. I snuck in and looked around. Everyone was sleeping. It was a crazy feeling. Like, of power. That I could do anything I wanted, if I wanted to. All I did was grab a vase and run out as fast as I could.

The dream.
The long hair in the drain.
The shrunken fly eyes.
The swollen face with the fish teeth.
The hands made out of wood.
The fingernails with fur on them.
    The protruding spine that ran down her back and all the way down her legs.
    Her feet. Her feet like big men's feet.
    A spider sitting in my lungs, building a web.

I started getting better at stealing things. First jewelry and electronics, then cars and cash registers. I almost never got caught. If there was someone there, I would make them swear not to tell anyone, otherwise I'd come back and hurt them. I made them promise. My mom and dad divorced around the time I turned seventeen. They never had another kid after me. I was their only one and I was an embarrassment. I think they didn't want another one, because of me. Why would you

want to chance having something like me again? They couldn't agree on what to do with me or how to fix me, so they just fixed themselves and called it quits. Quits meant they could finally take breaks from having to collectively raise me. That's the fucking truth that divorced parents of fuckups don't want you to know about. Mom could have a week off while Dad had me, then vice versa. I knew this is how they felt. Relieved. They didn't need to say it for me to understand that the end of their marriage meant the beginning of happier separate lives for both of them. Just because they made one mistake didn't mean they needed to spend the rest of their lives taking care of that mistake *together*. And so my anger grew stronger. My sadness. My demons went from renting to owning. I gave in.

Don't cry.
I'm not going to hurt you.
I just want us to have fun.
I'll be very gentle.

When I was eighteen I attempted my first bank robbery. It was a small local bank, but I got away with it. At least for a few hours. Because I had no priors and no weapon during the robbery, they gave me two years in a state prison plus parole. My mom came to the sentencing. She looked hollow. She looked defeated. My dad never showed. I think I disappointed him most of all, you know? He was the saddest of all.

I liked prison the first time I went. It felt safe there, and I was around other people who got me. We were all angry. We had all made one kind of promise or another, to someone or

something, at some point. A promise that got us here. That led us to this point, to this place of no return. In prison I got my first tattoo on my arm. I got a tattoo of my favorite model car when I was a kid, Curtis Turner's 1956 Purple Hog NASCAR Ford. See, I know *a lot* about cars. Especially racers. But more than the cars themselves, I know a lot about the men who raced them. I loved Curtis Turner model cars because I loved Curtis Turner. He was the only driver to win two Grand National races in a row. The first driver to qualify for NASCAR with a speed of over 180 miles per hour. The dude got the chance to work with the king of all mechanics, Smokey Yunick. The dude dreamed up, then built, the Charlotte Motor Speedway. He was . . . everything. Most of all, though, he was a comeback kid. Turner spent a lifetime trying to get more money and rights for drivers and formed a new labor union to support and protect them. The head of NASCAR at that time was a blood-hungry piece of shit who banned Turner and other drivers from NASCAR for life for unionizing. My boy went bankrupt. Became a drunk. Went dark and set up shop. But half a decade later, they lifted the ban and he was able to race again. And he had a major comeback . . . until his plane crashed in 1970. He was in his forties, I think. Crashed right here, in Pennsylvania, about an hour and a half from where I sit right now in this cell.

Over the next two years in jail I got a lot of cars inked on me. 1982 DeLorean DMC. 1962 Volvo P1800. A Ferrari from the '70s. A Pontiac Firebird Trans Am. I was going to get them all colored up and nice looking when I got out. Right after I got a job and a place to live. That's what I was going to treat myself to. But I never really made it that far. I

got out of jail on my twentieth birthday. I needed something to sell so I could make some money so I could get back on my feet. It's hard to get work with a record, you know? So I broke into a house. I just wanted to grab some jewelry or something, wasn't looking for trouble. I didn't know anyone was home. I started going through some drawers and this woman comes up behind me and attacks me. Starts hitting me and all that. But man, she was small and I wasn't—I'd been lifting weights in prison. Anger got the best of me, you know? Those demons. That promise. I threw her across the room. She hit the wall and fell to the ground. I looked at her, lying there in her nightgown.

She was just a normal woman.
She had brown hair and brown eyes.
She wasn't pretty. She wasn't ugly.
She wasn't really old but she wasn't young either.
She was just a normal woman.

Do you know who I am, I asked her.
No, she cried.
Good, I said.

I'm not proud of what I done. What I did to her. Throwing her on the bed and doing those things to her. I didn't mean for her to die. I swear to you. I just snapped. I don't know what came over me. I was on top of her, and her face . . . I couldn't shake the promise. I couldn't unsee the nightmare. I felt like she was laughing at me, even though she was crying at me. I put my hands around her neck. Remembered the bathroom.

Those hands on me. And I just lost it. I squeezed as hard as I could, until all the sadness was out. Until all the grief wasn't there anymore. And when I was done, so was she.

I PLEADED GUILTY TO MURDER. GUILTY TO AGGRAVATED ASSAULT. Guilty to robbery, to breaking and entering, to being a failure, a bad son, a piece of shit, a monster, a criminal. I pleaded guilty to keeping that promise. I got life without parole.

LAST MONTH I ASKED MY CELLMATE, SAL, TO PUT SOME NEW INK on my neck. For the last two years I've been in here, I've thought a lot about what I've done and what was done to me. I'm still young, you know? I still have a lot of life in front of me. I want to change things, but I don't know how to start. Wouldn't know where to begin. So I asked Ronnie to put some names on my throat. I put my mother's name, Lois. I put my father's name, Jacob. I put Arthur's name. I put Rezzy, for my child self and all that. I guess I was thinking they could hear me this way. They could hear me talking. And so at night I would talk to them. While lying in bed or whatever. I would talk to them. I would tell them things. Mostly that I was sorry. That I didn't want it to be this way. That I wanted a different life and that I was sorry I hurt them along the way.

I talked to my dad a lot. I could feel him there, on my throat, close to my voice. One night while lying in my bunk, I started talking to him, and I just said it out loud. I told

him. I broke the promise. Said what had been done to me all those years before. My voice, man. I never heard my story out loud. And my voice just . . . closed up around the story. Like protecting it, or something. It burned. The words were just burning.

I told him that he should've known. He should've asked. I told him he should've tried harder—when I was ten years old and fighting other kids but said nothing was wrong—he should've kept asking. Kept trying. He should've made me break my promise, you know? He should've done everything he could. Why didn't you do everything you could, I asked him, lying there on my cot in the dark.

A week later, the mail came and I had a package. I never get mail here in prison, so it was a nice surprise. Once in a while Mom writes and tells me how she is and tells me she's worried about me and asks if I'm eating and all that. But this package wasn't from my mom. It was from the name Fisher, somewhere in Delaware. I opened it and found a kit for a 1969 vintage original AMT Buick Wildcat, modeled in yellow. There was no note. Just the model car kit. But I knew it wasn't from my mom because when they divorced she took back her maiden name, Miller. So it had to be from my pops, Jacob. Jacob Fisher. And it was. It was from him. He had sent me a gift in prison, after no contact for almost three years.

I thought, you know . . . maybe he heard me. Maybe my dad heard me in here, talking to him. So I spent the next week putting the car together. It was a beauty, man. A beauty. You should've seen how gorgeous it was. I sent it back to him along with a letter. In the letter I told him what had happened when

I was ten. It was the hardest thing I ever wrote. He didn't write back. Instead, he just showed up. He just came straight here. He cried. Put his hand on the glass between us. He told me he was so sorry. Said I should've told someone.

And so here I am. Telling you.

TWO

C ALLER, YOU'RE ON THE AIR."

"Hi Donald. My name's Sebastian White. Non-listener, I'm afraid. But first-time caller, so that's a plus! I've heard about your radio show, of course, but I've never listened because, well, I can't really take the liberal-agenda to-do list, but I DO appreciate the work you've done for survivors like myself. Anyway . . . I don't really know why I called in. You know who I am, of course. Don't need to rehash all that. I was tagged on social media a few minutes ago by people telling me about the young man who just called in to your program. I was able to catch most of his story. And I guess I just want to speak to him, directly, if you don't mind. If he's still there. Ezra, I want to say something to you. I want

to tell you how brave you are. It is not easy to be brave. This world discourages authenticity from infancy. It is not easy to do what you just did. It is not easy to just . . . speak. Or even to wait to speak, for that matter. I'll tell you something . . . You know, I told many people what happened to me immediately. I told the world. I wanted the universe to know. I wrote books about it, spoke on TV, gave countless interviews, used my anger as a way to create action. I told myself . . . I told myself that she was nothing if I showed her through those actions that she didn't affect me. That I was still the proud queen that I am. Get right back up, Sebastian. Get up and blow your worst enemies a kiss. And that's how I've always survived, you know? I've learned how to make a meal out of pain, how to brand my sorrow. I don't think I've ever said that out loud before.

"I want to say to you, you know, I wish . . . I respect your silence. That you took the time you needed and . . . and I respect that. I envy that, really. I mean, I've done what I've done and I dealt with it the way I did but, in the end, here I am. Here I still am. You know? It didn't help me, if I'm being honest. To write and talk about her so openly. It didn't help me to push through everything like that. But you are brave, Ezra. And listening to you today has made me think a bit about things. How vague, I know! Sebastian White Thinks About Things! What a terrible title for a blog. Anyway . . . Who among us is not alone, Mr. Ellis? Which of us has forgotten her? None of us. Not one of us.

"So thank you. That's all. Thank you."

THREE

THE PROSPECT TIMES

Opinion
January 14, 2026

AN INVOCATION
by Donald Ellis

This is an opinion page, but what I'm here to say is not an opinion. It is an offering. It is a letting. A delayed release. An invitation to the beginning of who you are through the end of what you were. My name is Donald Ellis and I am not a survivor of rape. I did not survive.

I perished before pushing through. I had to end before I could begin again. My name is Donald Ellis and I am not a victim of rape. I am an assault's legacy. An embassy of expirations. I am the remnant of memory. Collateral debris. I am an earned epilogue.

Ten years ago, I was having a beer with a friend after work and a few hours later, I was violently assaulted and left for dead behind a dumpster. No, worse—I was left for living. My assaulter wanted me to *live* through what I had experienced. It was a gesture of torture, a most excruciating gift. I became suicidal. I told myself I did not deserve love. My children. My wife. I was an isolation of shame. A pending avalanche. I was blood outside its body.

Many times I have asked myself what I could've done to protect myself that night. I asked myself if I had deserved this. I convinced myself that I did, and it wasn't hard to. I live in a country built on celebritizing its citizens' grief and amplifying stories of violence and assault for political gain, click counts, or television ratings. Let me be emphatically clear: They. Don't. Care. About. Us. People who live through sexual assault are a crash on the side of the road, and the American media is nothing more than cars slowing down just long enough to take a peek. Just long enough to take a picture before speeding off to their next fatality. We are a country that capitalizes on the fetishizing of felonies. A country that says "innocent until proven guilty," even though the proving of assault is nearly impossible. Tell me how you prove coercion? How you

prove the difference between being hit on and hunted? How you prove your arms were held down? Your body was touched? Your life was threatened if you ever told anyone? For people who have suffered violent sexual crimes, proof—the very act of proving—is more than just a burden. It is boundless bearing. An eternity of futility.

I'm not one for witchcraft, but I believe in the power of spells. In the potential of many voices speaking at once in order to finally be heard. To force change upon those who are unwilling to do the hard work to help us. So if you were once left for living, like I was all those years ago, join me. Say it out loud with me now:

I am in a body. It is not the one
I came here with, but it is the one
I'll leave here in.
I will take care of it. It belongs to me now.
My pain, I will take care of it. It belongs to me now.
My heart, I will take care of it. It belongs to me now.
My story, I will take care of it. It belongs to me now.

I experienced death
but I am not a ceasing.
These hands remain sorcerers.
This mind contains many moons
pulling gravities.
Every memory is an ocean,
every remembrance a tide.

I have the right to recede.
I have the right to swell.

And though I am estranged from the sun,
I am a brightness,
lit from within.

With this voice,
I cast out the shadows.
My forced curse.
My executioner's oath.

I cast out the crime of me; my casualty.
Silence, you must leave.
Sadness, go.
Surrender, shame.
Cruelty, quiet now.

Only light now. Flair now.
Glow now. Radiance now.
Beam now. Blaze now.
Spark now. Gleam now.
Grow now.

I stand with you as you stand with me,
A mending before us and between us.
This body is my own. It belongs to me now.
My pain, I will take care of it. It belongs to me now.
My heart, I will take care of it. It belongs to me now.

My story, I will take care of it. It belongs to me now.

Ending, elapse.

Beginning, come.

X

ONE

EDWARD_DISPATCH: Hi Maude, my name is Edward Altman and I'm a reporter for the *Dispatch* newspaper. A former journalist for the *Dispatch* by the name of Joshua Greenfield reached out to you for comment almost a decade ago, and while he no longer works for the paper, I wanted to circle back now that so much time has passed and see if you would like to give us a statement or comment regarding the recent allegations of Ezra Fisher, who came forward with a physical description of you, which has, of course, reopened the case.

Is there anything you'd like to share with the public, Maude?

<Maude is now online.>

Yes. Look closer.

EDWARD_DISPATCH: Oh . . . You're here. You responded Hi. Hello. Look closer at what?

Use your imagination.

EDWARD_DISPATCH: What am I looking at? What am I supposed to be seeing, Maude? Sorry but can you—

What isn't she?

What space does she hold?

What do you think of her?

To whom does she belong?

What does she deserve?

What has she earned?

EDWARD_DISPATCH: I'm sorry, I don't . . . I don't know what you mean? Can I ask you some questions?

Shut the fuck up, I'm talking.

EDWARD_DISPATCH: Okay. Okay I'm listening.

I'm going to tell you some secrets. You like secrets don't you, Edward?

EDWARD_DISPATCH: . . . Yes. I—I like information pertaining to secrets . . .

I thought I told you to shut the fuck up.

EDWARD_DISPATCH: Yes. Quiet now.

Good boy. I have some questions for you, Edward.

EDWARD_DISPATCH: . . . Should I answer them? . . .

No. You should think about them.

What color is she?

Is she a mirror?

Are you in her?

looking at another figure?

What could be better about her?

Why are her arms shaped like that?

Do her arms remind you of your mother?

Do your mother's arms remind you of a daughter?

What do you want to do to her?
If you could do anything you wanted to, what would you do?

Play with her? Penalize her?
Hit her? Rape her?
Beat her? Cry on her? Cum on her?

Take her body away from her? Cut off her hair? Give her to your father? Give her to the government? Close her legs? Close her lungs? Burn her in public? Take away her children? Take away her abortion? Give her a miscarriage? Give her life? Would you cut off her clitoris? Cut off the parts of her face that don't match? Ask her to cut off the parts of her face you don't like? Cut out her carbohydrates? Inject her with something? Make her listen to something? Explain something to her? Show her how something is done? Indoctrinate her? Teach her? Fuck her? Make her white instead of brown? Make her black instead of yellow? Make her yellow instead of red? Make her eat her own red? Never let her talk about her blood in front of you? Does crying make you uncomfortable? Does talking make you uncomfortable? Does looking into eyes make you uncomfortable? Would you live with her? Share a house with her? Give her your last name? Treat her with respect? Cheat on her? Cheat on her with someone younger? Someone's daughter? Would that not bother you? Lie to her? Curse at her? Call her *good girl*? Call her *monster*? Is she dishonest? Deceitful? Is she violent? Are you surprised? Can you trust her? What if you can't trust her? How will you feel if you can't trust her? How will you behave if you can't trust her? What will you do if you can't trust her? What does it say about you that she can't be trusted? Is she awful? Is she awe-filled? Can she do it all? Does she have it all? Is she not good enough? Is she a coward? Is she beautiful? Can you have her? What if you can't have her? How will you feel if you can't have her? How will you behave if you can't have her? What will you do if you can't have her? What does it say about you that she can't be had? Will you make her pay? Will there be consequences? Will there be a punishment? Will you let it slide? What if she's ugly but you need to fuck? What if she smells but

you need to fuck? What if she's gay but you need to fuck? What if she changes her mind but you need to fuck? What if she's a child but you need to fuck? What if she's your child but you need to fuck? What if she's in pain but you need to fuck? What if you're married but you need to fuck? What if she lets people die? What if she likes war? What if she's ungrateful and unkind about it? What if she asked for it? What if she runs for president?

How would you feel if she did the same things to you?

What if she wanted to play with you? Penalize you? Hit you? Rape you? Beat you? Cry on you? Cum on you? Take your body away from you? Cut off your hair? Give you to her father? Give you to the government? Close your legs? Close your lungs? Burn you in public? Take away your children? Take away your semen? Give you life? Would she cut off your penis? Cut off the parts of your face that don't match? Ask you to cut off the parts of your face she doesn't like? Cut out your carbohydrates? Inject you with something? Make you listen to something? Explain something to you? Show you how something is done? Indoctrinate you? Teach you? Fuck you? Make you white instead of brown? Make you black instead of yellow? Make you yellow instead of red? Make you eat her red? Never let you talk about blood in front of her? Does crying make you uncomfortable? Does talking make you uncomfortable? Does looking into eyes make you uncomfortable? Would she live with you? Share a house with you? Give you her last name? Treat you with respect? Cheat on you? Cheat on you with someone younger? Someone's son? Would that not bother her? Lie to you? Curse at you? Call you *good boy*? Call you

monster? Are you dishonest? Deceitful? Are you violent? Are you surprised? Can she trust him? What if she can't trust him? How will she feel if she can't trust him? How will she behave if she can't trust him? What will she do if she can't trust him? What does it say about her that he can't be trusted? Are you awful? Are you awe-filled? Can you do it all? Do you have it all? Are you not good enough? Are you a coward? Is he beautiful? Can she have him? What if she can't have him? How will she feel if she can't have him? How will she behave if she can't have him? What will she do if she can't have him? What does it say about you that he can't be had? Will you make him pay? Will there be consequences? Will there be a punishment? Will you let it slide? What if he's ugly but you need to fuck? What if he smells but you need to fuck? What if he's gay but you need to fuck? What if he changes his mind but you need to fuck? What if he's a child but you need to fuck? What if he's your child but you need to fuck? What if he's in pain but you need to fuck? What if he's married but you need to fuck? What if he lets people die? What if he likes war? What if he's ungrateful and unkind about it? What if he asked for it? What if he runs for president?

\<Maude has left the chat.\>
\<Maude is offline.\>

XI

The sky above is disfigured with color as I reach the top of the subway stairs, where a homeless man asks me for change, his dog tied to a pole by a handkerchief. Poor dog. I have money on me, but I'd rather keep it. I don't mind his suffering. I prefer it. It's nice to be back after so much traveling abroad. Maybe I'll walk a while and enjoy the crowded streets near Times Square and the billboards covered in the ghoulish portraits of television's women. I'm in no hurry. I've got nowhere in particular to be. The fall is easing in and everyone's traded cardigans for coats. This is my favorite time of year. When everything begins to die without choice. When the great mother begins her grand death-sentencing. But I am the greatest mother of all. And while I'm not a murderess, I do love a good ending to a man's mind, especially if I've written it. It's not revenge. It's not payback. Nothing was done to me. It's just something I like to do now and again.

I'll make my way north up Broadway, toward Central Park. I've heard the benches are always filled with curious people. I've heard trees don't cast shadows there anymore because the sun sets first over the buildings that surround them. I think that was in a poem I read once. When I get there, I'll ask someone if it's true. Any man will do.

ACKNOWLEDGMENTS

I am writing this from the waiting room at a hospital where I'm about to get an MRI to see what I did to my lower back. Writing takes its toll. This book would not have been written without the support, love, and guidance from the following:

My literary agent Anthony Mattero. Thank you for your belief in me as a writer and your continued support.

My editor Laura Brown, for your bull's-eye notes and your kindest of darts. What a joy it was to work on this with you. This book is ours.

Amy Baker at Harper Perennial, thank you for being this book's guardian angel.

My finder, Calvert Morgan. Thank you for planting the seed.

Thank you Amanda Pelletier and Lily Lopate at Harper

Perennial, and Alla Plotkin and ID-PR for their tireless work helping to birth this novel into the world.

Thank you to the eyes and hearts and healers who stayed open throughout the years it took to write this book: Emily Wells, April Jones, Ben Foster, Thomas Sadoski, Gideon Yago, Mish Way, Katie Jacobs, Derrick Brown, Dr. Mary Bayno, Lisa Love, Moussia Krinsky-Raskin, Janet Fitch, America Ferrera, Amy Poehler and Mindy Nettifee.

Thank you, Evan, for your voice over the phone and your eyes in person, when we can.

Thank you to the organizations which supported and aided my research: Jay Wu and the staff at the National Center for Transgender Equality, RAINN, and Professor Michele Dauber.

Thanks to the phenomenal men who voiced these stories for the audiobook: Ben Foster, John Roberts, Glenn Davis, Jason Ritter, Marc Maron, and my papa, Russ Tamblyn. I'm extremely grateful. Thank you, Suzanne Mitchell, for your care in producing this audiobook. Thank you, Barry Crimmins for having lived and having given all that you did.

This book is also dedicated to my mother, Bonnie, my fourth grade English teacher Laurel Schmidt, and my daughter, Marlow.

ABOUT THE AUTHOR

© Katie Jacobs

AMBER TAMBLYN, author of the critically acclaimed poetry collection *Dark Sparkler*, has been nominated for Emmy, Golden Globe, and Independent Spirit awards. She has published two additional books of poetry, *Free Stallion*, winner of the Borders Book Choice Award for Breakout Writing, and *Bang Ditto*, an IndieNext bestseller. Tamblyn reviews books of poetry for *Bust* magazine, is poet in residence at Amy Poehler's Smart Girls, and is a contributing writer for the *New York Times*. Her work has appeared in *Glamour*, *Teen Vogue*, the *San Francisco Chronicle*, *Iowa Review*, *Poets & Writers*, *Pank* magazine, and elsewhere. She lives in Brooklyn with her husband and daughter.

ALSO BY
AMBER TAMBLYN

DARK SPARKLER
Available in Paperback and eBook

"An elegy, a eulogy, a rhapsody, a rage. In these astonishing poems inspired by dead actresses, Tamblyn fiercely examines the spectacle of the actress as she lives and dies and how our hands and hearts linger on their lives."
—Roxane Gay, author of *New York Times* bestseller *Bad Feminist*

Featuring subjects from Marilyn Monroe and Frances Farmer to Dana Plato and Brittany Murphy—and paired with original artwork commissioned for the book by luminaries including David Lynch, Adrian Tomine, Marilyn Manson, and Marcel Dzama—*Dark Sparkler* is a surprising and provocative collection from a young artist of wide-ranging talent, culminating in an extended, confessional epilogue of astonishing candor and poetic command.